T0348936

Sylvain Trudel

THE HARMATTAN WINDS

Translated from the French by Donald Winkler

archipelago books

Copyright © Sylvain Trudel, 2005

English translation copyright © Donald Winkler, 2025

First Archipelago Books edition, 2025

Le Souffle d'Harmattan by Sylvain Trudel was originally published
by Les Allusifs in Montréal, Québec, 2005.

Sylvain Trudel's *The Harmattan Winds* is published
in cooperation with Le monte-charge culturel, an
international literary agency.

All rights reserved. No part of this book may be
reproduced or transmitted in any form without the prior
written permission of the publisher.

Library of Congress Cataloging-in-Publication Data
available upon request.

ISBN: 9781962770224

Archipelago Books
232 3rd Street #A111
Brooklyn, NY 11215
www.archipelagobooks.org

Distributed by Penguin Random House
www.penguinrandomhouse.com

cover art: Emily Carr, *Blue Sky*, 1936, oil on canvas,
93.5 x 65 cm, Art Gallery of Greater Victoria

The publication of this book was made possible, in part, by the National
Endowment for the Arts, the New York State Council on the Arts with the
support of the Office of the Governor and the New York State Legislature,
the Hawthornden Foundation, the Jan Michalski Foundation, the Carl
Lesnor Family Foundation, and by public funds from the New York City
Department of Cultural Affairs in partnership with the City Council.

PRINTED IN CANADA

If you destroy the shadow of your tree,
you will seek that of the speeding clouds.

THE HARMATTAN WINDS

One

HABÉKÉ AXOUM, he was the smartest of all because he had
no guile and for him anything was possible. It's that he'd
kept his secret powers daisy fresh, just like me I have to say,
that's how I have eyes to see. So the broccoli on my plate are
elms, the mashed potatoes a castle, and the brown sauce is the
moat's muddy water. The sauce's beans are crocodiles to scare
off your enemies. In the castle there's a radish that rules the
kingdom, and a tower where a small marinated carrot I adore is
being held captive. Me, I am Goodness and Justice, and I want
to kill the radish because he's rich and the peasants are dying
of hunger. And he's impure and I hate him and I blast him with
peas from my catapult-spoon. Then I grab the pepper grinder
and sift snow onto the castle, lower the portcullis's tines, bite
into a crocodile in my path, and kill the radish, which emits
a sneeze. Lastly, I climb into the tower to free the marinated
carrot and I swallow the castle, the elms, the crocodiles. I leave
nothing on my plate, no remnants of the ancient kingdom,
no trace of what that world was so I won't have to suffer for
no reason, but you can't kill memory really and after dinner I
thrust the carrot back into its vinegar tasting of tears.

I often root around like that on my plate, despite my age, and people keep giving me odd looks because their eyes aren't sharp enough to see my kingdom. When you heap up years inside your head then the real takes up so much space that you blind yourself to the invisible and your kingdoms all collapse. Then comes adultery and hypocrisy. Adultery is the adult era where a childhood past is locked in rock. It breeds glaciers and the loss of mammoths. A glacial winter dulls your powers and it's the beginning of the end. Old age lodges in the hollows of your bones.

There was once a perfect example, King Midas, who transformed all he touched into gold. But despite the fact that his wish was God-given, the king was sad because even his bread turned to gold and his water became golden water and was no longer drinkable. Midas in his folly had tainted his dreams, and in the end he forsook all the gold in the world just so he could recapture his innocence. He washed his hands in a river, the Pactolus, and his gift left him, losing itself in those waters. Today the Pactolus flows golden, in memory of that king. King Midas with all his powers didn't know how to mature. Unlike Habéké Axoum, who has always been mightier than kings. When he was very small Habéké went fifty days without eating because of the famine, yes, fifty days, ten more than the king of kings called Jesus Christ, who was tempted by the devil in the biblical desert. Me, when I saw disasters on television, I wondered why we had to send food over there, given that Africans had bulging bellies. I didn't know that food has nothing to do with big bellies. It's Habéké who taught me that when the belly is empty it gnaws away at whatever's around it because a stomach never stops working, thanks to its juices. When the stomach is empty there are still muscles surrounding it, but once the muscles are eaten away they can no longer guard the organs inside them and the organs all want to escape. That's why bellies bloat.

If Habéké came into my life, it was thanks to the pure water he invented to survive. At the time of which I speak, Habéké was no taller than three buckwheat pancakes but he already knew how to make his own water when the sun seared Africa and Africans were dying off by the thousands. An army of cameras was filming all that because it was a horrible spectacle.

Later, Habéké would sometimes tell me about Zao, his sister Zaoditou, in his deepest voice, the one he had on bad days. Zao was so tired that at the end she didn't even have the strength to shut her eyes. She stayed like that one whole day without blinking, under the flies, and they had to be closed for her, those eyes.

At night Habéké hauled himself to the hilltops because he knew about the amazing insect that opens itself to the night wind blowing in from the distant sea. During the day it's pointless because the wind arrives from the desert, but at night, there it is, chock-full of humidity, like a breath, and when the wind glides over the insect's warm shell it deposits a dew. After one or two hours a precious drop slides down the shell to the insect's mouth and at last it drinks. That is how Habéké survived, on his belly, offering his lips to the miraculous night winds. The water condensed in his curly hair and ran down his cheeks to moisten his mouth's arid lake. Habéké tried his best to explain the insect to his family, but no one believed in his childish ideas. And this incredulousness led them all to die of thirst. The war didn't help, it must be said, because yes, there was a war among men thereabouts, which aggravated God's drought. The explosions were so terrible on the firing lines that even the guardian angels flew off at full tilt along with the birds, leaving the children bereft. Fortunately, there were, here and there, some valiant people who defied God and the war, bringing aid to the populace, dreamers who sent Habéké across the sea with endorsements and official documents, and that is how a friend dropped from the sky like a hair into my soup, into our physical world, with its peace and abundance.

On his arrival in our rich, frigid country, Habéké had a mere nine springs behind him, and so it was still possible to reshape him for his own good: he was taught French, hockey, baseball, bicycling, good manners, and *O Canada*. He learned to deposit coins every Wednesday in the children's bank account in his school's gymnasium. He discovered below zero Sundays on a skiddoo, nauseas in a sugar shack, the sheep, not even black, on the last float of the Saint-Jean-Baptiste Day parade, and television, where people who looked like him died on the news to make us ponder a bit before the eleven o'clock Western. And Habéké saw real-life nativities taking shape in front of his church, was called dirty names on the way to school, vomited hot dogs, tourtières, and yule logs, regurgitated Coca-Cola through his nose, caught chicken pox, choked on the body of Christ, and who knows what else? But Habéké, hunched down in his negroid heart, was able to resist our outrageous civilization, because, despite the invasions and deformations, he had decided to be forever an African in his soul just as a rock is hard. All his life he thought in Amharic, as he had promised his much-loved ancestors he would secretly do. No one could gain access to his thoughts because thinking is exile and each of us owns the exile he desires. Habéké and I, we vowed to pay visits to our respective exiles one fine day.

I loved Habéké. He had a human intelligence.

In Africa, the savannahs are teeming with zebus, but their leather is used to make shoes. It's sad to think it's our footwear that is responsible for the exile of the zebus. That hit Habéké hard, because he was an animist.

8

Two

A s FOR ME, I didn't exist until I was six months old, because up to then no one wanted to be bothered with such a case. Just my luck, I was not an official being, since there was no trace in the records of my coming into the world. Born by the side of the road like a natural disaster incarnate, I had not known the holy oil of baptism, and no one had thought to scrawl my name on a government document or anything resembling it, nor even to take an ink print of my tiny foot for a hospital data sheet, even if it was as cute as a tiny goblet. In short, no one dared to believe in me even if I was born bottoms up, like everyone else.

For a long time I believed that a hypothetical first mother had refused to make me her own out of human weakness or despondency. I imagined her despairing, seeing my ugly mug, and scurrying to the nursery to be reimbursed, or to trade me in for a cute little girl with doll's eyes, but it couldn't be done because the poor bewildered mother had misplaced the invoice. Which is why there existed no proof of purchase to vouch for my humanity. One thing is certain, I was not the fruit of Adam and Eve's imagination, I well and truly existed in flesh and blood, but I was neither attractive nor virtuous, because I was, deep down, alone. I no longer have any intention of moldering alone in my corner, and I hope to bear fruit myself one night, if a woman of the opposite sex should consent to bond with me. Céline, my adaptive mother, who adapted me to put to right a sequence of adversities, never wanted to directly broach that sensitive subject, because she had too many thorny truths to hide from me. When I asked her about how I came into the world, she leapt from pillar to post. I tried to coax her back to the pillar, but she stubbornly clung to the post. Happily, I had some friends who were able to enlighten me, Habéké in particular. He told me that for a very long time, even in Africa, life had been a total mystery because fertility could not be explained. It was an occult phenomenon and there are sculptures that depict this ignorance. One day, in the library, I leafed through a book filled with statuettes of black women with big bellies, enormous breasts, and little else. They are called attributes if I read it right, and they're symbolic; they represent the dream of a man who is reflecting on fecundation.

According to Habéké, man has a little aquarium in his entrails with microscopic fish that paddle around inside, and when a man eats, crumbs fall deep into him to nourish hope. Later, these fish become too big for the aquarium, and seeking freedom, they swim toward the light at the end of the tunnel. If at that moment the man is uniting with the woman, a series of locks leads the fish to the Great Lakes, deep, very deep into the heart of the feminine continent. Only one among them reaches Lake Superior, it's mathematical. It metamorphoses and its fins become proper limbs, its lidded eyes appear, its fish tail vanishes into the coccyx, the gills leaf out into little lungs, a tiny human heart, like a wild strawberry, starts to beat through the skin, and there you are, it's a child, no more, no less. When it has enough energy, this child parts the lake waters and escapes through the woman's contractions, but you must not blame it for its birth, because to blame children for their resolve to appear magically in the world is to deny what must exist, whatever bad feelings there may be. Myself, I'm against prohibitions, stranglings, cuttings, and other demeaning things. In Africa they have this diminishment, they amputate bits of people. If I were an African my fathers would have chopped off my foreskin, because the foreskin is seen as the feminine face of the masculine medal, and these medals mustn't have back sides due to ancestral beliefs. And if I were an African with a sex, this is another deep mystery of which I would have been deprived. Gustave Désuet wrote that "the sensitive parts of religions are in principle beneath the belt." He was terrible, Gustave Désuet. I loved him a lot because in a sense he helped me to live my life, but he will never know that, he's dead. Gustave Désuet was a man of letters in the plural because he had a lot of them, as you can see on the back of his book. He was a sort of paper tiger who one day took up his pen as you would take up an arm to do evil, and poison dripped from his nib. A real viper, that tiger. He said that we, the rich of America and Europe, we're living in the Accident, curled up in our accidental countries, and the Bible's Apocalypse is a great idiocy because it has already begun and no one sees it, it's ongoing right under our eyes that choose to run and hide behind their lids, but it's there, and in fact it's us, yes, the Apocalypse, it's ourselves, we are the cataclysm of the poor, seeing that we kill them with one hand hidden behind our backs in the convenient darkness of our heads, so as to stay rich at their expense. We can say what we want, but what we do in the shadows, or what we allow to be done given that it fattens us up, well, that buries everything, really everything, the exquisite principles along with the corpses, and it's charming that way, the accidental civilization, so charming that it doesn't even perturb our sleep. The Accident had in fact inspired a Gustave Désuet poem called "Conjugation of the Past Decomposed."

> *I Soviet Union*
> *You United States*
> *He Third World*
> *We bourgeois far away*
> *You snore*
> *They die*

Gustave Désuet knew the pain of living and he loved love, which is why he died young, as you might expect. I had one of his books at home, *Dreamed Lives,* a collection of poetry, but Gustave Désuet wrote "poesy," like "rosy," because that gave it an élan. This book lived under my pillow. Céline had bought it for me, reluctantly, at the flea market where it smelled of mould, but I wanted it at any cost.

"What are you going to do with a book like that? There aren't even any pictures."

As if I just cared about pictures, but one picture is worth only a thousand words, no more, because a picture is flat, it only has two dimensions so it hides the invisible, which is no longer free. While in Gustave Désuet I could sense the infinite as far as the eye could see and as far as life could go, I saw the unknown that transcended me and cast light upon me, as in the first poem I read, "Oh Woman of my Silence," encountering it the way one life enters into another.

> *I bitter old man*
>   *and I ease myself into the night*
> *I am solitude*
>   *in fields caressed by the wind*

With surfs of fetish cries
  in gardens of death
And my memory is hollow
  as frigid earth
And I bemoan the flaxen path
  of your sacred burn
Oh a life in torment
  rain on the yielded house
Yet yesterday still
  I was todaying forever after
We were a morning of scents and murmurs
  and I remember the freshness of sounds
But see I am far from that world
  oh woman of my silence and my secret
I magnifisense your eyes of blackened gold
  and I love your face that is no more
While there rises in the east
  my neuroses' sun
But it is death that rises thus
  in a life's light
And I lament all you were
  all the stars in your mouth aflame
But in weeping I shine
  like a gemstone's tear
And I am pure at last I am pure
  and I am forgiven for having lived
Oh holy wounds you anoint me
  with a woman's blood and you bless me
I am pure at last
  pure forever from having been loved.

Of course, we didn't understand all those brightnesses
flung off from the head of Gustave Désuet, we often felt like

small birds before the ocean, but we hid ourselves here and there, Habéké and I, to read passages out loud, then we tried to understand what it was all about. We loved the path of the sacred burn, the pure blood of a woman, the pain of a man alone, and today being a verb; we felt we could understand that the world is the world on condition that we be the world as well, I mean both in it and around it, from nothingness to infinity, never closing our eyes on anything, neither happiness nor despair, to suffer and understand suffering, which is perhaps in the end the only goal of life. Of course, we hid the book because we feared that our parents would forbid us this bad company that taught us lamentation and discontent, but that was unfair to Gustave Désuet, who only wanted to transform our poor perspectives into enlightened states of mind. He said that the infirm, the obese, the sick, the poor, the unhappy, the old, and the wanton are like all of us, they also want to feel desired. This is important, because if you do not feel wanted, you're an island so small that you are not on any map.

Three

A T THE AGE of six months I was shedding frigid tears, forgotten in a broken-down supermarket cart. My first mother, with whom I'd had a glancing acquaintance but whose whereabouts on earth are unknown to me, had expunged from her life her child of ill omen, and the cart was bobbing like a crayfish cage in a bog of bulrushes by the side of the highway. Trapped like a small animal, I was dying of hunger, thirst, and solitude.

It was then that Céline Francoeur turned up. Spotting an infant flailing the air behind cattails and bulrushes, she hit the brake pedal to halt this attack on the universal rights of children. Bereft of everything, I was shivering on the rim of the cosmos, suckling in the void a breast I had never seen, or perhaps the moon which I took for the Great Bear's udder, when I was suddenly lifted into the sky. Céline took me in her arms and was touched to the point of wanting to make me a permanent part of her life. For the runt that I was, permanence was a dire need, because you have to take root far from the temporary if you're going to have a future, given that the temporary is of short duration; and too, without milk and caresses there's no warmth, and by extension, no life with its tenuous hopefulness. Céline was not all alone as a better half, as Claude, the other half, also showed himself to be partial to a desperate cause, just like Saint Rita, despite my crossed eyes, a bit almond shaped, unlike his own. Céline and Claude had just slipped rings onto their fingers, till death do they part, and for them it was a bargain to come upon a little baby fresh off the production line. They could have all the benefits, right off the bat, of that indescribable joy, minus nausea or miscarriages, as long as no one went to reclaim me from the lost property counter. At the time I was certainly happy in my obliviousness and puniness, but with today's eyes open to what is around me I personally find it unjust, because they knew full well that someday they would have their own children, their own little purebred loved ones. That meant that I, this entity, would forever be the lost one of the family, the stray mutt stumbled on out in the open, the little ill-starred bastard son of nobody.

I learned of this sombre story one night when Céline and Claude thought I was asleep, but I was not sleeping at all: I had crept up to the master bedroom where they were arguing. There, in one fell swoop I was plunged into the darkness of my unknown origins, and I came to understand that I was an eternal thorn in their sides, because the turtledoves had never agreed on the significance or the import of a secret sorrow I had harbored forever. She insisted that she had wanted to tell me everything from the very beginning, so as to ground me in the truth and to see me flourish, whereas Claude swore that it was best just to pretend all that didn't exist, that everything would be okay. In the end Céline and Claude canceled each other out and shrouded my solitude in the silence of the night that saw me born. It was simpler that way, and besides I was certainly oblivious to everything, no it was impossible, I couldn't be channeling the cruelty of an ancient sadness dating from before I even had a memory; there was no unhappiness deep within me, no phantom pain. No hint in my heart of what had poisoned my first days on this earth. No, it wasn't serious. It was enough to each Sunday light the candles for Saint Rita and let my natal sadness rise in smoke like incense for the angels as the flame cleansed my wound. No, there was nothing to fear, I was nothing.

So it was that from one day to the next I became an orphan, Claude and Céline became my semi-parents, Jasmine my semi-sister, Benjamin my semi-brother, my bicycle my semi-bicycle, and me in my corner I became the semi-member of the household.

Four

E VER SINCE THAT NIGHT, the night my foreigness was revealed, everything had changed inside my head, and it was all changing faster and faster without the semis suspecting. The air was electrically charged, and my aggrieved heart filled with poison. I was wary of my shadow and stumbled over the merest unfamiliar word—and I monitored my helpings of mashed potatoes in case they might have shrunk in order to adjust themselves to the new restricted space I inhabited. Jasmine and Benjamin were too young to appreciate my family drama, and I didn't blame them for having growing appetites that matched their larger portions of potatoes. But my life was no longer what it had been, it was as if I were haunted by the muffled cries of great black evil birds.

And then, one night, there was an incident in the living room that altered everything. On TV, experts in neurosis and other chronic afflictions of modern life were discussing lost orphans who delved down, like the blind, into a genealogical darkness, seeking their secrets. These tales of human origins were of great interest to me, but Claude, reluctant to face home truths, chose to switch to a less hazardous channel, where a mindless songstress was whinnying away. And I saw red. All flushed cheeks and bloodshot eyes, I slammed my fist down onto the plate of chips, scattering them every which way, even into the curtains, and even onto a startled Pipo, after which I knocked my glass of Coca-Cola onto the carpet. Poor Claude, wide-eyed, froze at first, comprehending nothing, but it didn't take him long to become inflamed.

"What's got into you, you goddam little bastard!"

Throwing himself upon me he seized me by the wrist, gripping me vise-tight to the point of cutting off my circulation, and wielding his muscular arm he planted a five-fingered flower in my face. The worst thing was that I understood him, and that in his place I would have done likewise, I would have whopped him as hard as I could to pummel his flesh and his mind as well, but already, in advance, I was forgiving him for everything, and embracing the pain that was being dealt out man to man. Until suddenly a single drop made me burst my banks, when Claude spat out the worst thing he could have said, when he called me a son of a bitch. Time stopped dead in the living room, fear hung heavy in some invisible medium that bound us together, a silence come from afar, from a place where we are strange to one another, and I saw that I was poised on a turning point. Céline was framed like a still life in the living room door, Céline said nothing to defend me, and that drove me mad with rage because it would have been simple for her to do something for me in that moment of death when I was alone like a dog in the universe, no offense to Pipo. It all ended when I went to weep tears of blood into my feathered pillows.

That night I came to understand that the insides of rootless men are steeped in exile. These new thoughts had me brooding in my bed, but I told myself that the walls of silence would one day come down because not all the mammoths were extinct, there was still one that burned brightly, and he was hiding inside me like a will to survive what ordinarily kills. Then I began to think about Habéké, the most uprooted of us all, who was showing the way to all the lost souls of our world, and I felt that he would be a brother to me, no offense to Benjamin.

In Africa a hot dry wind, the Harmattan, blows desert sands over farmlands, killing trees, flocks, villages. The harvests cease to be, despite there being more and more mouths to feed, and people suffer, because chewing on sand amounts to nothing. To live, it's clear, you must correspond to something. Pipo, when he yelps or leaps for a biscuit, corresponds to a frisky dog. Jasmine and Benjamin, when they play hide-and-seek or wet their beds at night, correspond to children. But me, with my almond eyes, when I ravage chips and Coca-Cola, I correspond to nothing, certainly not a normal son.

In our house I corresponded to everyone's guilty conscience, the same for Habéké, who corresponded to all the naked Africans poking their heads through the TV's window at night on the news, eyeing the food steaming on our tables. That's what set my semis to trembling in front of Habéké, who by his simple presence seemed to denounce the entire Accident. Because Habéké bore within him the black peril of a foreign world where everything is threatening. Because Habéké, who stayed to eat with us, was the TV image come alive on a chair at the end of the table, over a full plate, a kind of phantom who lapped up super-hot soups that burn mouths not used to food.

In the end, I corresponded to Habéké, who corresponded to Africa, who corresponded to the primitive, which corresponded to the dawn of humanity, which corresponded to the distant and perhaps ill-fated morning when Céline Francoeur found me in a grocery cart.

It was with that sodden cart that the infernal cycle began, as on one of those many days empty of meaning.

So powerful was my feeling that I corresponded to Habéké that I decided one night to write him an urgent letter, asking him to invite me to his cottage for a few days. His parents liked me fine, and I told myself that there would surely be no problem. And so I licked a bad-tasting stamp, applied it to the letter, and sent off the envelope, postmarked with my hopes.

Five

W HEN HABÉKÉ AXOUM turned up in our small town after years in Montreal with his adoptive parents, he made waves. I have to confess that Habéké, who came from Africa, had people talking thanks to a shortfall in our overall preparation and his own strangeness. It was the first time that a genuine Black had appeared to us in the flesh, outside the television set, and we, the young Whites, wanted to touch him with our fingers to see what it felt like. It was clear that this boy had soft chocolate skin, woolly hair, bright eyes, a boxer's nose, teeth like piano keys, and long long legs held together by bony knees. He pronounced his French better than we did, and his name was strange. And he wore around his neck a beautiful necklace of blood red carnelian, and on his wrists magical bracelets to bring on the rain. He beguiled me when he described the women where he was born with their blue gums and hair agleam with Suri butter, children from far away who stuffed coins into their mouths as into a little sodden purse; and then Habéké talked about smoked milk, crepes made with black flour, red pepper that stopped hair from growing on your tongue, and of Egziabehér, which over there is God's name. He also told us amazing stories, such as the one about the serpent Wollou who swallowed up young girls before granting wishes, the one about bad coffee that was poisoned by Abyssinian sorcerers and ravaged your intestines, the one about the leper whose fingers were eaten away, and whose rotting tongue was sliced out of his mouth by his mother, wielding a wild dog's shoulder blade, the one about the prophetess with lightning eyes, perched in a terebinth tree, who saw in her gourd of honey the birth of a black Christ, or the one about the tiny evil sprites who slide down the sun's rays.

All that is to say that I liked Habéké right away, without the normal hesitancy with new people, in case they didn't turn out to be like what you thought. Yes, I liked him, unlike all the big twits on the school bus who knew nothing at all about different peoples.

One morning, Habéké was greeted by a few idiots who paraded their doltishness everywhere they went.

"Howdy, big blackie toasted on both sides!"

"How much do you cost, slavey? Do you have all your baboon teeth?"

"You'll never find a girl around here, your asshole race isn't long for this world!"

They spewed their poison right in his face, but Habéké had not yet said his piece.

"We blacks, we are the good Lord's beauty spots."

I thought he was brilliant to have answered back like that, and I asked him to be my friend for life. He said yes, but without a lifetime guarantee. Because he had wisdom in his blood, that devilish Habéké. From that point on we became the index finger and the thumb of the same helping hand, and everything that touched him touched me and vice versa it goes without saying, because brotherhood always works both ways.

Happily, Habéké lived nearby, so I could see him going out every night with his legs, because he could run for hours without tiring. His endurance and his breathtaking legs were beyond imagining, and I thought this was related to savannahs and leopards. One day I posed the question, delicately, so as not to wound his pride, but Habéké was not sensitive on the subject, and he explained that in the plateau valleys it was the hyenas and the panthers that inspired fear, then he said, "All parents believe in heredity until they realize that their children are idiots."

One day I learned that his great-grandfather had once been a fabulous runner during the hunts, but he had been sacrificed like a measly chicken by some scumbags. It all happened at the turn of the century, in nineteen hundred and something, when his grandfather worked for the Europeans, building a railroad. At first the rails were going their own sweet way, until one day a foreman, an Italian apparently, or perhaps, it was said, a German, unless it was a Frenchman, but in any case a filthy bastard, dispatched a rail car packed with penurious workers so as to assess the stability of a bridge. Suddenly everything collapsed in a chaos of wooden beams, and the Africans vanished. The torrent at the bottom of the ravine swallowed up the clues to the mystery that might have loosened tongues and sent the culprits to prison, but they all pled innocent out of racial brotherhood. Alas, the torrent can't talk despite the blood that reddened its waters, but at times it rumbles loudly when the rains revive its anguish, and its thunderings are the accusations everyone hears, but far too late. The poor great-grandfather lost his life in that catastrophe, but he passed on his extraordinary legacy to Habéké, beyond mountains and the vastness of time that comes between modest men, and it's a little, for this lost ancestor, like a reawakening of his blood, a triumph for his fiery soul fluttering its wings in a realm of wonder.

Habéké sprinted along the railroad line that mounts northward, snaking through our landscapes of lakes, rivers, and hillocks, certain that one day he would arrive in Africa, and would find his ancestor at the turning point of a life. For Habéké thought he was still alive. He saw him in a dream, wandering along rail lines somewhere in the world, beyond the horizon's blue seam, singing his laments to pass the time and nourishing himself with dreams from the land of his birth, his milk and his honey. That is why my friend ran, imbued with his faith, trailing in his wake sorrows vast as the wooded steppes, as unending as the Horn of Africa, and charged with sadness.

One night, as I was picking raspberries along the rail line, I saw in the distance the bronzed silhouette of Habéké, walking in sadness, and it so moved me that my plastic bowl tipped over and my small fruits fell to the ground. I trampled them, those beautiful raspberries, to humble a little the loveliness of a world daring to burst forth in the gold-tinged twilight, but ignoring my friend.

I remember that I loved talking with him about Africa, and that is why I know some things today, for example that Africa is a stew of languages and that Habéké's is full of burgeoning vowels or that in Africa men's problems, due to their galloping demography, are both acute and grave, high-pitched and low, therefore circumflex, making Africa a kind of quotient, for it is, according to Habéké, the product of divisions between peoples, and over there that's all there is, peoples. From east to west, the African sun shines down in its passage on Somalis, the Danakil, the Toubou, the Ngambay, the Mboum, the Yoruba, the Peul, the Soninké, the Éwé, the Baoulé, and then the weary sun goes to die at the end of its tether in the home of the Wolofs, not to mention the Boos, the Bobos, the Toucouleur, and the Tupuri. There exist, however, little hooded hats made of soft rubber to rein in the ardor of the peoples, but that's no solution because those are foreign remedies, not well attuned to the circumflex dilemmas of Muslims or animists. And then those rubbers look like the moltings of snakes or little caimans, and I'm wondering what a man of this ilk would do with such a device, he who reveres the companionship of sacred pythons and crocodiles. And as Habéké brings to my attention, no one down there sees why one should couple if not to reproduce oneself eternally, to procreate in the universe, whence the comedy of the missionaries and their vows of chastity, incomprehensible in the eyes of the Blacks who see the world through a different eye, their dark eye if you will, whence also comes the fact that the sorely beset missionaries must sometimes invent invisible wives that shadow them everywhere like lambs' tails right into their lice-infested bedding, so they swear, to earn respect in that domain.

All of which is to say that in Habéké I found an echo to my own life's problems. I had thought of myself as the only person born into that pea soup stew, but when I learned of Habéké's implausible existence, I saw in him a brother in arms, my kin in improbability and the darkness of things. And one day, sitting on a bench in the old railroad station, I told him about my calamity in the bulrushes, my botched birth, my lost invoice, my semi-family, my other man's eyes, and all and all, and he touched my hand with his. It was black on white, like writing, and even, you could say, like a girl, because Habéké was soft to his fingertips, but no, it was not quite that, it was something else but I don't know what exactly, perhaps friendship as you rarely find it, and perhaps that's why, when by chance you encounter it in the course of your life, you don't know how to name it. Yet to invoke eternity you must somehow do it

26

justice, to extol its human warmth, you must make a sacrifice of our sun's flesh and blood. On the day of which I speak Habéké and I pledged eternal fidelity one to the other, and we buried some coins beneath a railroad tie, to represent a priceless treasure. Never mind what life held in store for us in its great injustice, there would always be those coins slumbering, awaiting our return, to bear witness to the two of us in the light, to everything we treasured, to our hopes and all those things belonging to the secret man in whom we had faith.

Then Habéké excused himself to rise on his thin legs. All pensive and still moved from having been understood, I watched my friend move off toward the horizon where the railroad line bends, where the Africa of his dreams and of his human suffering endures, where the complaint of his great-grandfather drifts in the infinite, where the trains buried beneath the sadness of years have come to rest.

I ended my first letter to Habéké with a poem by Gustave Désuet, which he had composed out of love for the only woman in his life he'd ever adored, which did not prevent him from living unhappily and dying alone at the age of twenty-nine, hanged under a wooden bridge, in the countryside, his toes dipped into a stream. When some children found him, the poet had already been devoured, in part, by birds.

> *Go, my friend,*
> *I do not know who I am*
> *But go and sing the amity*
> *Of the beasts you calm*
> *Unceremoniously,*
> *Oh my friend*
> *Across the planet*
> *All is smaller than you*

And I know you to be the cedilla
Beneath the canine consonant
Of my encaged heart.

Six

I WAS ON THE BALCONY with the air of a bear in a wrought iron cage, my legs prickling as if assailed by hot ants, because my shot in the dark had not fallen on deaf ears. The brave Habéké was flying to my rescue. The previous night my semis had settled the fate of their wayward child, and they liked the idea of sending me off to gambol in the countryside for two weeks, breathing in pure air and calming my aggressive tendencies.

Suddenly a station wagon as big as a hearse turned the corner. It was him, Habéké, and I grabbed hold of my little bastard's tiny valise. A moment later I was in the Godin's car, laughing with my friend and teasing him to beat the band. While we fraternized man to man, his parents chatted with my semis, who were leaning against the car door. It took a while, but at last we got on the road and the house and family slipped past the window like fleeting dreams. I took in the little group I was leaving behind me, Céline and Claude on the sidewalk, Jasmine and Benjamin on the balcony, Pipo on the lawn, and suddenly I choked up as if I were seeing them for the last time. They didn't know that I knew everything they knew, and they thought they were living a normal life, but there was secret knowledge befogging our view and imposing between us much that was unseen. I saw them as innocents, innocent children who'd not yet learned that things can go awry. That day I knew that my life had begun, despite them and despite me, to drift away from them. I was born of an unknown star and they had had the goodness to rescue my wildflower, but I was now too blatant a presence in their décor and I had to retreat to my star, bearing with me my singular scent. I saw their hands waving as if I were heading off to die, and I stopped making fun of Habéké who, sensitive as he was, saw me morphing into someone not the same. I kept my eyes on the bustling city, teeming with children shouting and playing ball, oldsters warming their legs in the sun, parents like ours trailing a burdensome brood behind them while their eyes worked hard to hang on to a remnant of peace. I don't know why, but beyond all that I saw a sadness that takes your breath away, the sadness of everything that endures only for a season, like a dream or all the frailty latent in things. Yes, truly, my heart was riddled with holes like those in your pants pockets, and all my life's savings were seeping away. To close a wound you need only the blood it has spawned, but how to ease a pain that seethes and eats away at you out of sight? Feelings cause you pain, spear you with fire, penetrate flesh and bone and tear open the heart, they can impale a man as if he were a doll, whatever the last chance entrenchments may be that he calls on to shield himself.

As I was pondering this human gloom I was being shunted from city to countryside, to where houses were sparse, where the sky opened out onto all matter of infinities, where the road was increasingly indolent and less impatient to get where it was going, and where you could also smell cows. With all its bullrush ditches and metal post boxes like armored helmets gleaming in the sun, this road was charming. It ran through placid valleys bordering a modest river, through a landscape of farms and grain fields where feelings themselves might ripple and sway. Vast shudderings swept through the corn stalks on their way to the ends of the sentient world, mimicking my state of mind at this instant of my life. Far off, under the umbrella-like elms reminiscent of Habéké's African acacias, cows grazed beneath the sky.

It was then then that the car slowed to leave the road and entered a narrow lane beneath the weeping willows' leafage, a pebbled lane bordered by glowing lion-hearted daisies. The chalet appeared in the windshield with its window screens, its honey cake chimney, and its roof of sandy shingles, like frosted sugar.

"Here we are, boys!"

We opened the doors with gladness in our hearts. The warm earth with its plants smelled good and we heard the gurgling of the blackbirds who seemed to be crying "Uncle Henry!" We walked on the tips of our toes so as not to disturb anything and we went to touch the river that streamed, cool and swarming with life, through our fingers. I remember the wind in my hair, Habéké's shoulder brushing mine as we took in the trees and the clouds. Cellophane butterflies came to rest on the bent bulrushes; everywhere on the water glided little x's, the skaters; fish mouths made circles, sucking up a bit of water along with the mayflies; and tadpoles squirmed in hollows of stagnant water.

I also remember the beating of my heart in this new world.

"I can't believe how beautiful it is here."

"You haven't seen anything yet. In the garden there's a Damas plum tree, a Babylon willow tree, and a Persian lilac, and also a well where you can get water from a pump."

Good god, I felt at home in this elsewhere at the end of the world.

"Boys! Come and eat!"

While we were marveling, Habéké's mother had made us a nice little snack, tuna fish sandwiches with salted cucumbers and Oka cheese. I found Habéké's parents very nice. They'd started to age a little because they had married late, but in their heads they were still playing hopscotch. We know that they adopted Habéké through international agencies, that's understood and it's all to their credit, but also, and there's no point sweeping dust under the rug, that Monsieur Godin had problems with his plumbing. The poor man didn't have fish active enough to sow Madame Godin's Great Lakes, so they lobbed a last chance buoy into the unknown, and it's Habéké who latched onto it.

"We're going to the village now. Do you want us to buy some melon?"

We answered yes, comically, in unison, because melon is universally delicious. And Habéké went so far as to ask for marshmallows to eat in front of the fire, as without them there is no countryside.

The afternoon rolled around, and we played at being explorers caught up in a prehistory overrun with terrifying creatures, where we were waging a fierce war against pterodactyls. It was just for fun, but in the course of the hostilities a pterodactyl really did collide with a milk truck making its way along the road. Seeing that, we ran toward the drama to lend a hand, and there, tucked into the clover to die in peace, we found a poor robin convulsing. As there was still a hint of electricity in its wings, we thought all it required was a good shock to set the little blood machine in the bird's heart to running again. So we carried the robin into the chalet where we plugged its feet into a socket, but that seemed to be a non-starter: the bird came out dead as a doornail and on our conscience.

To repair the harm we had done we devised a funeral service that would apply a bit of religion to the wound, but

Habéké insisted, in his particular state of sadness, and since he was still an animist, that it be on the trunk of a poplar tree, and by its Holy Ghost wings, that we crucify our corpse. Then Habéké set fire to some twigs and prostrated himself before the robin, chanting prayers in Amharic wherein he offered excuses to the bird for having embarked on the pterodactyl hunt. As for myself, so as not be bogged down in unbelief and inaction, I ran to find Gustave Désuet's poems, and I recited a strange text that I didn't understand, but that was called "Mortality."

> *Your head*
> *Coiffed traitress*
> *Proud*
> *Of the spider diadem*
> *That crowns you.*

We mourned in the shadows so as not to disturb the sanctified soul that could now rise up freely into the purified firmament, safe from the souls of pterodactyl hunters, cats, and those of milk trucks.

Before leaving the crucifixion site, Habéké snapped open his pocketknife to disembowel the bird. I asked him why he would perform such an astonishing act and Habéké replied that in Africa the soul becomes a bird only if the body's blood is drunk by the tree, if the bones blend in with the bark, and if the marrow becomes the flesh of red fruits.

"This must be done," Habéké told me, "in case that bird turns out to be one of the eight great ancestors incarnate in the tatagu kononi..."

My mouth fell open and stayed there...

"Um, okay, but what's a takagaykonomie..."

"The tatagu kononi are the firebirds venerated by my people."

It was touching to see this deep-seated faith in such a slender boy. Habéké was, in a sense, a very pious man.

Soon after, we went to wash our hands in the river and shower each other with ideas. Under the dock, in the clear water, I spotted something that looked like a sea serpent.

"Habéké, look, in the reeds, an eel!"

We wanted to eat fish, so we took a branch, and made a crude harpoon. We almost fell to arguing over who would launch the missile, but Habéké, generous to a fault, left the honor to me and to my status as a guest.

A bit clumsy thanks to my lack of wilderness training, I went to position myself on the end of the dock, where I looked like a small decorative god of the hunt. I stared the prey down to hypnotize it, then I split the water with my perfect arrow. That stirred things up in the environs, but once calm returned we saw that the eel had made off into the deeps of his sunless world without a scratch.

"I told you to be careful about the illusion..."

He meant, the little genius, the angling of light rays through the surface of the water, and his rebuke went right to my swelled head, which was very well developed for a little brat my age.

"Okay, enough! Leave me alone, you and your angles!"

"Hey, if you start acting up, I'll send you home by the seat of your pants!"

He told me off in no uncertain terms, this dear foul-mouthed Habéké, but in fact he was right. In the first place, if I'd been fair, I would have let him proceed, he who wanted to impale the eel and make me happy, and I'm sure he would have harpooned it scientifically, that unfortunate eel. Secondly, If Habéké knew how to make the school bus imbeciles choke on their idiocies, he was strangely unmanned when it came to us, his friends, as if the thick skin he presented when faced with such challenges frayed in the close quarters of comradeship. In other words, Habéké was saddened by the raised voice of a friend, and I had hurt his feelings on that dock. I think his sensitivity derived from all that had burdened him since the flameouts of his birth, and that they stoked his fevers: cherished individuals gone from the earthly kingdom of things, but who dwelt within him like ghosts, like apparitions that stirred beneath the surface of his being, souls that glided across his skin, because Habéké was himself an empire of elixirs... He walked, his head full with charred landscapes and human shadows, and one wondered where he headed, weighed down by so many catastrophes. Clearly, in those days, I did not yet see things that way, so Habéké and I sulked, but the absurdity of it all soon nipped our childishness in the bud, and afterwards, ashamed of ourselves, we made up, no harm done.

Later, after supper but before the marshmallows, I felt out of sorts and went to lie down. I wanted to blame it on the fried chicken we'd eaten, but I dozed off and had a nightmare. It began with a vision of the crucified robin twisting about on its tree, wrenching out the nails, and flying off into the night to enter the chalet through the chimney. Then the robin laid an egg in the sleeping Habéké's mouth, Habéké swallowed the egg, and the baby hatched in his stomach. Just then, in the river, the eel wounded by the harpoon gave birth to a baby eel that snuck away through the water main. After appearing in the kitchen faucet and corkscrewing itself out of it, the little eel crawled to Habéké's bed to slip in turn into my friend's mouth, and that's how the fish and the bird were able to devour Habéké from the inside. I saw in my dream my friend crying out and writhing in pain, then his belly ripping asunder. The mad bird flew into my face in a volley of feathers to gnaw at my eyes, and I felt the beak and claws rooting in their sockets. All sorts of disgusting liquids ran down my face and into my mouth, acid blood and bitter eye juice, and I went blind. Suddenly I felt the eel climbing up my body like a snake, right to my nose, which it entered through a nostril. Gluey and cold, it curled into my throat, and I awoke with a jolt, all in a sweat.

"There, there! Calm yourself, it's nothing, everything's all right…"

Madame Godin was bathing my face with a cold washcloth. Poor her, she must have thought I was seeing ghosts, but I was still frightened, lost somewhere, because part of the dream still lingered within me, like swathes of mist in the night.

"Where's Habéké?

"He's gone for a walk outside."

I shook my head as if to fend off a hallucination. Then I stammered:

"The eel… the bird… Habéké…"

"Oh, you're running a temperature. I'm going to get you an aspirin."

But fever is for horses, and with Madame Godin gone I vanished in a flash. I decided I was feeling better, because it's better to be cured than to call a doctor.

Outside, the field grass through which I was sprinting soaked me to my knees, but the day no longer reached ankle high to the night, and the stars were dropping one by one into the river as if to foul it. My feet were thumping ahead of me all on their own, I was running freely, parting the rustic fireflies. I thought, in my flight, that Habéké must not die. We had too many kingdoms to conquer for us to yield to a death that would lull the world, and within me I felt an enormous need for him, my life's close companion, while in the darkness, in my flight, I saw the future.

"Habéké, where are you?"

I ran along the road, keeping pace with the moon behind the trees, and that encouraged me. All at once, far ahead, I detected a miniscule darkness darker than the night, a darkness shaped like a man, and I recognized the silhouette coming toward me on its familiar legs. It was my Habéké, undevoured, Habéké, true to himself. As we met in the moon's ashen light, an island rose up from the shadows about us, an exquisite isle of night. On this island where no man had set foot, I saw the hopefulness of the despairing in search of a land free of memories, where they might plant their tree of life.

"I dreamed that you had been devoured by monstrous creatures."

Habéké was panting, which was strange given his legendary endurance, but it was his excitement talking. "I went... over there...," he said, pointing his finger into the night. I let him catch his breath, and then he told me that he had explored a railway line overrun with crickets, near the village, beneath the moon. His eyes gleamed in the darkness, and it was clear that he had seen something special.

"I think I saw my great-grandfather."

I didn't dispute him, wanting to give his miracle a fighting chance, and I promised Habéké that we'd go back the very next day if he wanted, because I too wished to see him. And did he want it! He would have dragged me by my hair!

That night, on the star-filled trip back, I had a revelation. Habéké and I may not have been milk brothers, but we were blood brothers certainly, and that was something we had to celebrate.

"You know what?

"No, what?"

"We should marry..."

*

37

I HAD TOUCHED a sensitive nerve with my aspirations and my idealism. The next morning, with the sun in our eyes, near the water and its thousand blooms, Habéké and I scoured the undergrowth, seeking the essentials for our marriage, bound by blood and our candid, pure beliefs.

In a pot borrowed from the kitchen, (called a casserole by Habéké's mother, a "presto" by mine), we began by stirring two handfuls of native earth into water from the sacred river. (We told ourselves that the entire earth was native everywhere and for everyone, given that we are all born somewhere, so it all comes down to the same thing because of the roundness; and it's the same for water, sacred everywhere, because water is an endless cycle of storms and evaporations, and a drop born during the rainy season in Africa could easily link up with the sea one day and cross the Atlantic, to at last rise into the American sky and rain down on other peoples, that's why men are everywhere baptised with the same rain universally renewed.) Two mouthfuls of water to be precise, spat right away into the pot, to purify forever the words we would swear...

We then had to find the tatagu kononi sap that alone could link our destinies to the origins of peoples. For this, we went to extract the nails from the poplar's robin. This was not easy; it was as if its bones were starting to bind themselves to the heart of the tree. Then we plunged the tatagu kononi into the pot and doused it generously with sacred mud, our word made flesh, and we lit the celebratory fire. Clouds of smoke lifted into the leaves, and we coughed, but it was beautiful to see the sun's rays slanting over our heads. After the coughing we set the pot into the fiery bouquet and, while this spiritual nourishment was on the boil, Habéké and I renewed our vows of lasting fidelity, the promises we had made at the old railroad station, with Habéké's black hand over my white one. We pulled the pot out of the fire when the steam began to shriek through the little steel cap, and it struck me that Madame Godin would not be pleased: her beautiful casserole was charred and the handle had melted. When we lifted the cover our eyes met the robin, whitened and in part liquefied, afloat in the putrid juice.

"We're missing the most important ingredient..."

Uttering these words, Habéké took out his pocketknife and sliced each of us in the chest over our beating hearts. The blood we collected we mixed with the nutrient broth warming over the ritual flame. We ground up the tatagu kononi with a rock and tossed the carcass into the woods. All that was left at the bottom of the pot was a brown, reeking liquid, but Habéké and I weren't bothered by that because this moment was so significant. And so that our beliefs would be properly set in motion and would penetrate to the very marrow of properly swathed individuals, we stripped naked in the middle of nature to steep our bodies in the warm soup. With my finger as my paint brush, I adorned Habéké with mythic decorations, on his arms especially I inscribed zigzags, the trajectories of spirits who come and go between earth and sky, the visible and the invisible, then I covered his face with a calcinated ancestral mask, because Habéké was a scorched figure of Ityopya, as described in the encyclopedias. I depicted as best I could pythons on his legs, then a giraffe, and an antelope, and a lion drinking from a lake in his navel—the lion for courage, the giraffe for greatness of soul, the antelope for purity and quickness. Afterwards, Habéké daubed me too with the creamy substance. He traced a tatagu kononi on my face and drew a tree with branches on my arm, leaves on my hands, and roots on my legs down to the toes. It was a balanza, Habéké said, his Africa's supernatural tree that drinks the ancestral blood of the adored firebirds.

After the marriage ceremonies and the decoration of the participants with the magic liquid, we hid in the bushes, because the paintings had to last a whole day to guarantee us a modicum of eternity.

The morning passed without incident despite the ants, both literal and figurative, that set our legs to itching. The first problems appeared at noon, when the Godins began to search for us all over because our absence (as well as the casserole's disappearance) was starting to worry them. As nervous parents, they pondered the possibilities. The first thing that came to their minds was the river, because young people like us love to drown themselves in rivers. Armed with bamboo poles, they groped the thickets in case we may have died there, then finally came upon our behinds, and their eyes popped out of their heads.

"For the love of God, will you tell us what you're doing there?"

We came out of the bushes as naked as Adam, coated in a crust that flaked off with our every move. Clearly overwhelmed by what they saw, the parents couldn't possibly appreciate the ceremony we were enacting, and there would have been no point trying to explain to them that we were celebrating our lawful wedlock.

"Go and clean yourselves up right now, my little monsters!"

It was clear that the Godins had no truck with the beliefs of others that they couldn't understand. And so we dove into the river to wash off our decorations, after which Madame Godin, who in the meantime had retrieved her ruined pot from the coals, fixed us with a murderous gaze. Furious, she assailed us with blows from her bamboo rod, and then, exhausted from hitting us so hard, she demanded a reimbursement for her kitchenware, in a thunderous voice that made it clear that there was no hope at all for us to strike a deal.

Habéké and I were upset while we got dressed because we were wondering if our marriage was in fact legitimate, but also because a pressure cooker like that could cost about fifty dollars. Fortunately, we had a brilliant idea that energized us: we would take oysters from the river, who were living there peacefully in the familial mud, we would kill some of them while making our excuses and would prettily paint their shells, then we would take them from house to house, to the neighbors by the water, and return with piles of money raised for an artistic cause, just like others did. Habéké even bettered the idea: we would also peddle perch to fish lovers.

An hour later we were scrabbling under the water, harvesting oysters easy to capture because they moved so slowly, hardly at all. Soon our pail was brimming with beautiful bulging mollusks, and I was thinking, how strange is an oyster: like a live tongue concealed inside a powder compact.

After the shellfish chase, we set ourselves up on the wharf, and I laughed, because Habéké, with his straw hat and his fishing rod, looked like a little plaster black boy in a garden. We impaled some innocent earthworms, squirming in their death throes, on our fishhooks, then we trailed them along the sandy river bottom where the delighted perch allowed themselves to be seduced, at the cost of their lives. It was a real massacre, but one mitigated by our prayers. Soon a dozen fish were jiggling about in a second pail. The perches' green and gold cross-hatching posed a question to my witless intellect.

"In your opinion, can we say that a zebra is tigroid and that a tiger is zebraed?"

"Why not? Species get mixed up."

*

THAT NIGHT, at the end of a dizzying day that had just about killed me, just when I had no more expectations, Habéké's ghost entered my room and I'll never forget his lunar eyes.

"I'd like to show you a secret that nobody knows."

With my blanket pulled up to my nose, I was afraid of what I would see, since Habéké had pulled out a letter from under his pyjamas.

"One day I'm going to leave, despite my parents... I'm going to go back to the world from which I've come."

His farewell letter to his adoptive parents was already written, and I read the first lines by the light of the moon.

> *Dear second mother,*
> *Dear second father,*
>   *Once upon a time you saved my life and for that*
> *I thank you, but you did not really know what you*
> *saved or that you can only save a life for a very short*
> *time and one day there will come a time when the*
> *true invisible life will awaken and that day has come*
> *for me and that is why this morning you will find my*
> *bed empty and that...*

I did not go deeper into this letter, teeming with truth. I turned about in my bed to hide my face, and the ghost left me to go off and dream about the day it would see the light. I don't know what there is in a letter that so touches a man, even a young man, but I was moved from having read what I had always felt, that Habéké already, like me, had one foot in another world. I saw in his secret the true potential of our marriage in the bushes, the eternal vow we had murmured to each other.

That night I didn't sleep, I knew only the stars shimmering over the chalet and the river, over this dreamed-of life where

Habéké and I would go to remake the world and found a new people. Eyes wide in the night alive with crickets chirping beyond the window screens, I was levitating along with the curtains buoyed by a warm August breeze. Lost in revery, I reflected on the meaning of a life, and I concluded that it's not good to live alone, it's unhealthy, living alone means listening to oneself breathe in and out day and night until one becomes faint; it's to feel the echoing in one's temples of a heart beating in the void. And pondering so relentlessly on this heart, you feel it tightening like a fist, because a heart too doggedly observed wants to take its own life; and to live alone is to slowly stray into a desert where the soul ends up making a noise inside one's head like the gnawing of a rat.

As I sank further into solitude listening to the beating of my heart, I began to reflect on marriage between people, not my symbolic one with Habéké, but the more pervasive matrimony between men and women. I would have liked to know what it felt like to have a wife and children, to betray them and lose them, or perhaps to save them for a time without knowing what one is rescuing, and then to grow old and feel oneself dying in silence.

As I was turning over in my mind all these mesmerizing thoughts, Madame Godin was grumbling in her sleep in the next room, perhaps dreaming about our catastrophes, and her husband was snoring through his bulbous nose. I wondered whether Habéké's parents still sometimes loved each other, whether they kissed, eyes closed; then my thoughts strayed to another room in another world and I asked myself whether Claude and Céline dropped off to sleep just after sliding back to back between their sheets, their shoulder blades echoing the dark side of love, or if they at times still called on each other a little at night, when no one is the wiser, to assure themselves that they exist.

I thought also that they should have told me everything as soon as I acquired a memory so that I could live with it and get off to a decent start; or they should never have revealed this mystery so we could have wrapped our lives in a dark cloak of silence, with me living in an eternal night where this whole matter was concerned. But they had to choose the worst possible scenario, rife with discord and hidden agendas, where I was but a little bastard with no past or future, a pup without a leash foundering in the self-same oblivion from which he had emerged for no good reason, as if surfacing from a Pandora's box.

Yes, truly, to receive such news at such a tender age dealt a fatal blow to my present person, still waiting to be born.

Seven

A T DAWN THE NEXT DAY I was still having dark thoughts and a bilious heart, but mornings are so arranged that you never know whether they're coming or going. I was still able to get up on the right side of the bed, and it was worth it: when I went into the kitchen, Habéké was there in the sunshine wearing his stupendous smile.

"Hi! You want a glass of orange juice?"

I saw in his eyes that he was once more a man ahead of his time.

Oh Habéké of my silence and my secret being, as Gustave Désuet would have said. Oh Habéké of holy Africa, you were the wizard of my days, the little man who lent color to my grayness. I was up and about for only thirty seconds, but already I was smiling, and my heart was agog with an urge to live.

"Did you know that you talk in your sleep?"

Ah. Another truth that Habéké will have taught me.

"You mumbled strangely, as if you were praying."

And so at night I recite my sorrows like beads on a rosary, and I worship in darkness hordes of gods come down from the ceiling, but it gives you an appetite, such craziness, and that morning we ate crepes while talking low, because the parents were still in their own world, dreaming, and the house in suspension over the sounds it made. A plump negress presided over the box of crepes, Aunt Jemima, the Aunt Jemima of the Deep South, and that reminded me that the Blacks in the United States were called "colored." I learned that from Jackie Robinson, the famous baseball player, who said one day: "I'm not blaming God for giving me black skin, but I would have liked him to make it thicker." I told myself that I was colorless, like dead meat or celery water, and I envied Habéké his color, the color of Aunt Jemima and Jackie Robinson.

*

ON THE TABLE, among the jam jars, were scattered our creations. The oyster shells painted by Habéké were amazing, while mine were barely credible, poor little things. I did not have his gifts. Habéké's most remarkable creations included a white-tailed gnu and his beloved female, the gnu being a mammal of the savannah, a strange combination of antelope, horse, and bull, but the animal, deep black with a white tail end, seemed imbued with a dream's silvery loveliness, because the oil paint had been applied to the pearly surface of things, which could account for the effect, but certainly not his talent. On the commercial side, the shells were being sold for a dollar, as were the perch fillets, except that each fish was sold a flank at a time, which instantly doubled the profits, ideal for us and our blatantly commercial goals. To preserve the freshness of the delicate flesh, the fillets were stored below zero in a cooler, wrapped in newspaper that sullied our hands with its bad news.

And so we set out early in the morning with all our gear, for the chalets on the water's edge. Our first stop was at Monsieur

Aldéric Loiselle's. He was a retired priest Habéké had talked to me about, and he had shut down his parish while awaiting a young curate who needed some persuading, yet this priest still had a lot of religion in his voice and in his gaze, and in his hands as well, which were pale and human.

"Come in boys, what can we do for you?"

He said "we" as if he were not all alone in life, and I didn't understand what he was getting at, but finally I think he was right, because no one can do anything all by himself, and no one who has faith is alone.

"We are two young artists," ventured Habéké, "and we are trying to repair the pain caused to a poor lady."

"I see," replied the priest. "And who was responsible for this pain?"

"We were."

"And who is the lady in question?"

"My mother."

The old priest laughed, but was intrigued by our project, and asked us to show him our goods. We opened our cases, the two little Noah's Arks, and spread the shells out before his pious eyes, explaining as best we could what we had done.

"This is a pair of moose from our beautiful Canadian forests. The female is the shell with no antlers on its head because the antlers are used by the males in the lovemaking season since they have to physically impress the female who is more secretive and chemical in certain regions, but she is still sensitive to big animals who are in heat, just as in everyday life, and after the season of love they don't fancy each other anymore, like everyone else..."

The priest laughed some more, but I didn't see what was so funny, then he bought my moose and I was much honored by his confidence in me.

Then Habéké deftly defended his territory.

"Do you know what African animal most interests the missionaries?"

"Um... the lion?"

"No."

"The elephant?"

"No."

"The python?"

"Still no."

"Very well, I give up."

"It's the tse-tse fly. And here is a young tse-tse couple that will impress your friends."

The priest bought Habéké's giant flies, he really was very talented. And I had never seen a priest with so much money in his pocket. The good Monsieur Loiselle wanted to know what we were carrying in the cooler, and we replied "a delicacy for a fine palate." He had us open the cooler, and with his eyes agleam he bought two fillets, far beyond our expectations.

"You see, I have a kind servant," the priest told us with a wink that said everything, "a good sister from Sainte-Jeanne-d'Arc who comes to do my cleaning and ironing, and as she is arriving this afternoon I'm going to give her a big surprise with these perch fillets and some cream... washed down with a fine little muscadet nicely chilled..."

He suddenly seemed less weary, monsieur the priest, with a flush in his cheeks, and I thought it was due already to the medicinal effect of that fish, which is so good for your health thanks to its phosphorus. In the end he gave us six dollars cash down, so that Habéké and I felt ourselves getting rich faster than we'd expected, then monsieur the priest declared that we were good boys and even, with God's blessing it appeared, wished us greater profits. And invited us to return and see him again. We left him with some reluctance, but our reparation drew us on.

"He seems to have a lot of money, your priest, but I guess that's not a problem."

"I don't know, it's not my religion."

Habéké meant the Catholic church that presided over our community, not the pure apostolicism of the early days, with branches leading up to it through the liturgical Gu'ez language and the Coptic borrowings from the Blue Nile, bestowing on Habéké as a child some knowledge of the *Schla Maryan*, Image of Mary, and the *Gebre Mesquel*, Slave to the Cross, which he in no way questioned.

With the cooler that we carried together, we walked through the countryside, noses to the wind, our pockets full of coin. You can say what you like, but money lifts your spirits.

We sold the marvelous pair of gnus at the next house, to some young people who lived from fine herbs and pottery. The girl seemed wondrously beautiful to me with her loose hair that fell nicely, straw-blonde hair that veiled her jewel-like eyes. Her boyfriend was tall, red-headed, bearded, pony-tailed, and seemed very kind with his Sunday smile, his bronze-flecked eyes, his artist's hands, and his sandals fanning out his toes. They first listened to our sales talk, and then praised our shells. But what I liked most was that as they reached for their money they showered us with compliments. They bought the gnus, as I've said, and Habéké's leopards, zebras, impalas, hip-popotamuses, and giraffes, and even his lycaons, a kind of dog with ears that stick out. They must have bankrupted them-selves, the potters, because they also purchased the ugliest of my pairs.

"What does that represent?"

"Narwhals."

"What are narwhals?"

"They're marine mammals that give birth to unicorns."

"We'll buy them!"

They loved the plastic arts and the expression of feelings, but eating, not so much. They spurned our perch, and we left them in peace with their boring vegetarianism.

Before we left, they made us a friendship gift: a pot in the form of a piglet, to protect our savings! We thanked them warmly, and from there we hopped from chalet to chalet until we were out of stock, as we'd hoped. We sold everything in just a few hours, even my wolverines, which were pretty pathetic.

Back at Habéké's chalet, we emptied the moneybox that contained thirty-two dollars and smelled sweetly of fresh money. During the afternoon we did more fishing and created more masterpieces. The next day, our business brought us twenty-three dollars, which added to the thirty-two of the day before, meaning we could pay off the pressure cooker. Proud of our accomplishment, we presented a neat bundle of fifty dollars to Madame Godin, who couldn't believe her eyes, nor we ours, and then, with the wind in our sails like little businessmen whose appetite has been whetted, we kept our campaign going for two more days, enough to stuff our piglet with fifty new dollars, giving us a nest egg.

One night, Habéké and I went to explore the rail line with, in my bag, the little treasure we wanted to sacrifice to our ideal. It was a way, just between us, to abolish the Accident, since Accidentals can't comprehend that kind of sacrifice. Habéké was already far in front of me, given his legs, and I tightrope walked along a rail, under a moon that reminded me of a poem by Gustave Désuet, my only other friend, my best paper tiger.

> *Oh, how beautiful he is*
> *This downy little faun*
> *Who lifts to the sky*
> *His kid's horns!*

Habéké informed me that a kid is a little goat. He knew his zoology, Habéké, he knew what he was talking about, when he was a small boy in Africa he saw people applying cow dung to their wounds along with stomach juice from disembowelled kids. Incredible of course, but it's because it's far away, Africa, so far off that down there they don't have the same stars as we do. It's different constellations that make them dream, like the Virgin's Ear, the Sculptor's Studio, the Phoenix, and the Female Hydra; and then they have a different moon that tilts like the rocking of a cradle, a different sun that rises dizzily, vertically, straight as a flaming arrow, so much so that equatorial Africans do not know dawns or twilights, their day explodes around them all at once to dazzle the night, then their night, in the evening, falls like a bronze bell onto the day to snuff it out. Yes, it's very far from the world I know, this strange African world, and I don't know if one day I will be alive to go there, but despite the inconceivable distance that makes me tremble with fear, I can say that, with Habéké as my source, I have touched it a little, this Africa that touches me, and I have felt on the back of my neck it's life's exhalation, like its death's breath, and I can see that somewhere deep in myself, there where so many mysteries trouble me, I am this unknown, I am this fantastical continent that is adrift in my friend on the rivers of night, and I feel as though I am brushing up against a world of fire.

"Hugues! I've found my great-grandfather!"

Habéké was running, brandishing an object in his fist, a bit of wood that left me puzzled.

"Look! It's his pipe!"

"Don't be silly, that's not a pipe."

"Yes, it's a piece of my great-grandfather's baobab pipe, that means he's been here, he may not be far..."

Habéké began shouting into the night the name of the man of his dreams: "Dedjené! Dedjené!" and I heard a dog begin howling far off, answering the senseless echo. Oh, I too believed in his great-grandfather, but not that night, because this was not the fragment of a baobab pipe, and I waited for my friend's conviction, like a brush fire, to gutter out. I sat on a rail, ten minutes later Habéké saw the truth, and it stunned him enough to silence him. Then he came to sit beside me on the rail, an act rife with meaning. He'd had a spasm of hope that was unforgiving, and he felt foolish. We stayed like that for a while, listening to the crickets' song and the dogs howling across the countryside. A sense of calm settled over our shoulders while the moon's rice paper lantern lit up a vaporous cloud, and I saw the moon of Africa aglow, that jewel in Habéké's memory, the moon that, in Gustave Désuet's poetic madness, is an opal of King Solomon lost in the Queen of Sheba's navel, or the cuttlefish bone in parakeet cages where the birds of night sharpen their beaks before poking out the eyes of children who dream too much. Perhaps also this moon was the very soul of Gustave Désuet who, disguised in satin, *in the night paced his hectares of saffron.*

For a long time I sought the universe hidden in this pungent alexandrine, in those hectares of saffron, waiting for the russet moon to reveal to me the poet's soul.

"Do you think we're still young?"

Habéké had opened his mouth to draw me out of my revery with his anguished question, so deeply existential.

"Why do you ask me that?"

"Because I hope we're still young."

Habéké was filled with anxiety because he knew he was born in Africa where people don't live long, and an immense fear percolated in his blood like a sickness.

"Don't worry, my friend, we're going to be young for a long time yet."

Speaking these words, I had an inspiration, it was a telling moment, and I took from my bag our piglet full of money.

"Should we bury it here?"

Habéké nodded yes, and we dug a hole where we could bury our cache under a rail tie. We wanted to dedicate this money to an ideal alive within us, that of the poor who want no more of the world that is devouring them, nor of fears, nor of impotent lives, but who free themselves like ripe fruit to take to the sky where the miracle is to be found.

We wiped our muddy hands on our pants and left the spiritual circle of this new sacred site to wander through the wind laundering the sky, but Habéké, still beclouded by his age-old hopes, had to perturb the silence that was smothering him, and so he talked to me of his great-grandfather who was called Mekkonen, "the Noble," but whom Habéké named *dedjené*, "my defense," given the love he bore him.

That is how our steps led us onto the old iron bridge spanning the river, where we sat down to dangle our legs in the air. The wonderfully black water flowed beneath our feet and in its profound civility it returned a favor to the sky by reflecting back its newly awakened stars. The union of water and sky was so perfect that the horizon seemed to be the promise of a new age, an eternity for ourselves alone.

"Do you know where it's going, the river?"

"It's going out to sea."

"And does this river have islands?"

"I don't know. I've never seen farther than the village."

In me, a folly was starting to put forth shoots, and I was sure that Habéké would be able to merge this new life with his own. I saw the burgeoning folly's island, and it was our island, all abloom in an exquisite dream, and imbuing itself with destiny. It was a far-off land that would have to reshape the world from the ground up if we truly wanted to make everything over with our naked hands and sow new Americas and Africas in a garden of scents and songs.

"We're going to leave... we're going to go to an island... if you want to come..."

Habéké didn't reply, but he knew what I wanted to say. He would fly away with me because he too saw it, a sky that opened wide like a mortal wound, and there where the world bled there blazed the mirage of this virgin land where we would go to plant our balanza and our poplars, where robins and the radiant tatagu kononi would sing.

We stayed on the bridge a bit longer, watching the river run on with its curious furrows, as if it bore in its memory secret wounds, lacerations of the drowned, and I thought of the death of worlds, the birth of follies, and the exile of little ill-born bastards.

*

SUDDENLY, WITHOUT WARNING, slashing through the shadows, a train appeared. Bearing down on us at full speed, it was clearly not going to stop for us, and after my first startled reaction, I saw that our poor little lives were at stake. Leaping into the void was the only thing to do, and we did it just in time. The train brushed by us like a meteor, but we were safe and sound, hurtling down amid the wind and stars. Below, the river swallowed us up, and I was afraid of drowning in its dark water, but then our heads broke the surface. We still had a long swim coming, but happily Habéké knew how to float, more or less, though after a while I had to grab him by his pants to hoist him onto the grass.

Once we'd made it to shore we thought back on our misadventure, and I could hardly believe what had happened, or pull myself together. Habéké even wondered if we ever would. But it was then that I had another brilliant idea.

"Do you know?... If we'd had wings, we could have...!"

He got my drift at once. He had gauged what might be feasible and he saw what we would need.

If we wanted to fly off in the company of souls and birds, we had no choice: wings have always played a role in the soothing of malcontents.

*

CRAFTY AS THE SIOUX, we were careful to make no noise, because the Bessettes were having breakfast, and it was so quiet in their cornfields that they might have heard us. Simulating a tree's shadow, Habéké placed a stone in his sling. Meanwhile I crawled along the side of the chicken coop, skirting the sight line of the allegedly ferocious Monsieur Bessette. The chickens were pecking and milling about in the farmyard with no inkling of the drama that was unfolding, but as Habéké explained to me, he who was no stranger to chicken blood under the guardian tree, the fate of a chicken is more often than not to be killed.

Given all that, Habéké shot me a glance to tip me off that he was ready, then he executed admirably, and the streaking stone exploded the chicken's head, impressing me deeply. It was then, after the killing, that I went into action: armed with a rope knotted into a lasso, I had to haul in the murdered chickens. In fifteen minutes we managed to collect and slaughter four birds, but then the dog woke up at the end of his chain and began to yap. We feared for our defenseless behinds because Monsieur Bessette could easily fire on us with his salt and pepper ammunition, he had the calibre he needed, and such an assault would have had us dancing a merry jig. We took off, arms in the air, fowls in our fists, corn in our ears, and I wondered if Monsieur Bessette could see, through his window, his dead chickens soaring over his corn at the ends of four long thin arms, two of which were as black as a cast-iron frying pan—that would have given us away.

Back at Habéké's we plucked the birds, and that was another butchery, as we'd never tried it before. By the time we were done we had feathers even on our eyelashes, but not enough to fuel our mythic project, so we went to steal one of Monsieur Godin's pillows, raiding it for its down. Later, at dusk, our suspicious silhouettes crossed the road, heading for the far end of the buckwheat field where we wanted to free some trays of honey from their hives. Once there we wrapped ourselves in mosquito netting, leaving two holes for our arms.

"Are you ready?"

"I think so..."

"Okay, lift!"

I raised the hive's roof, heavier than I thought, and Habéké took hold of the bees asleep in their honeycombs. My friend was able to slide one layer into the bag I was clutching in my teeth. Successful, we decided to repeat the delicate operation so as to double the quantity of honey, but a gust of wind blew the second bag away.

"Hurry! The shelf is slipping!"

"I can't find the bag!"

"Quick!"

The honeycomb fell to the ground and the bees had a rude awakening. At once, we fled towards the chalet with our single layer of honey in hand, but as we were running flat out the mosquito netting came loose, to the delight of the bees. By the time we got to the chalet, we were swollen all over. As we were applying vinegar to our stings, Madame Godin appeared on the scene.

"Are you the ones who cut up the mosquito netting in the shed and emptied out Raymond's pillow?"

We didn't deny it, that would have been futile.

"Ah! Little devils! That'll cost you twenty dollars, my friends!"

We painted more oyster shells and killed more perch.

*

THE POLLEN-FILLED AND BERRY-SWEET air hummed with horseflies and deerflies.

Next to the railroad bridge, amid a blizzard of dandelion seeds, I was sticking the last of the chicken and pillow feathers onto Habéké's long arms with our bee glue, while my own skinny arms were longing to spread themselves wide in the firmament.

"Okay, your wings are ready, but what are we going to do if it works?"

"We're going to perch on the big tree, over there."

"All right, but don't forget, we can't fly too close to the sun."

As we took to the bridge, we received a barrage of insults from a handful of young slackers haunting the riverbank.

"It's going to rain buckets, the chickens are ready to perch!"

They showered us with jibes, but Habéké and I went about our business calmly, our eyes fixed on the horizon, solemn in our well-nigh biblical roles, advancing to the middle of the bridge where we halted, there where the night train had surprised us as we were dreaming about being reborn. Then, after one tentative step forward, poised on the brink of nothingness, we raised ourselves on the tips of our toes and extended our long, honeyed and feathered arms. The time had come for

57

us to change our nature, to fly off and reign under other skies, far from the Accident and its false promises, and it's then that in one and the same breath we launched ourselves into the void, beating our arms. My eyes were closed, the better to see the miracle, and I believed in it so strongly that I would have sworn that we had taken to the skies, but I was deceiving myself in no uncertain terms, and once again it was the river that doused the flames of our humiliation.

It was the young good-for-nothings, in a fisherman's rowboat, who dragged us out of the feathery broth.

"Why did you jump off the bridge?"

There was a hint of respect deep in their eyes, but we evaded the question.

"You're crazy! You're sick!"

We left them with some strong impressions, but in fact we were snot-nosed, half dead, bereft of both island and sky, and drenched to the bone. We went back without saying a word, trailing our embarrassment along the shoreline paths, and it was Madame Godin, her again, who saw us coming out of the bushes.

"What have you done now, my rascals? How is it that you've messed up your clothes again?"

"Because the river was full of water."

Madame Godin found us pretty pathetic and we were getting on her nerves, but I leapt to Habéké's defense: if there had been no water in the river, we wouldn't have gotten soaked. It was like the story of hats. If hats didn't exist, men wouldn't have heads.

Exasperated by our fraternal silence, Madame Godin whupped our rear ends with her thirty-six-inch cane, that's an imperial yardstick, an English yard.

"When you come right down to it, my little devils, I don't know why I'm even bothering to hit you. You never get the message, not in your behinds, and not in your heads!"

A little later, rubbing our backsides to ease the pain, Habéké whispered into my ear.

"Parents are like that: if you ask them about their private life, you get a whack, but if you don't answer when they ask you about your private life, you get an even harder whack!"

*

THAT NIGHT, I let Habéké know, officially, that I wanted to sign a mutual assistance treaty with his Minister of the Interior. Habéké went off in his slippers to consult his ego, then sent me a supersonic telegram. On the airmail stationery I read: "Of course, dear so-and-so, the minister and his signature await you." We played the fool talking with long-legged words so as to mock the bastards who feed off human sorrow.

Later, we read Désuet, who brought us home to what's human.

> *The dying man*
> *comprehends*
> *a sun that trembles*
> *seeing the child being born*
> *phoenix of the eternal cry.*

Like two mirrors placed one in front of the other, Habéké and I pondered the infinite. Before going to bed we had signed, all the same, in the presence of the defunct Gustave Désuet, a Geneva Convention that would bind us one to the other if the sun were ever to flame out.

That night sleep eluded me once more, and I took advantage of that to reflect on the phoenix's eternal cry. That's how I had the idea of being reborn from my ashes on the farther side of things. I jumped up to wake Habéké and to talk to him about China where everyone must plant a tree during his earthly sojourn, where the Chinese worshipped swallows to the extent of eating their nests in their soup, all of which inspired me to think about life, given the balanza and the tatagu kononi.

"I'd never thought about that, but I'd love to go there to see if I'd be a happy man..."

I wondered whether my unknown father's tiny eyes perhaps came from China, just like jade, and me as well from the same silk road. Listening to my follies despite the late hour, Habéké was inspired, and we got more and more carried away: we imagined ourselves already in the middle of a field with our shovels, shoulder to shoulder, digging a huge hole beneath the clover to emerge in China at the bottom of a well, in my promised land perhaps, on the far side of the sea and the Himalayas. What was most wonderful was that there was no mutual assistance obligation in our Geneva Convention that would take us there together, to this empire where there perhaps lived another me, there was only the friendship between peoples, which pleased me enormously.

*

THE NEXT DAY, we spat into our hands under the Babylon willow tree, armed with our garden shovels. Before opening the earth, we apologized to the underground spirits, promising to fill up the hole after our arrival in China, and our excavation began at around seven o'clock. At first we dug away gaily, telling ourselves that we could hardly wait to see the first rice roots appear, I was dying to see my own eyes looking back at me from the bottom of the hole, the freshly quarried earth smelled good, and the pile of it was growing apace. According to Habéké's learned calculations, we had seventeen days of hard labor before us. We expected to end up in Manchuria, but we dared not alter our direction for fear of coming out under the Yellow Sea: the Asian waters would then empty themselves onto this side of the earth, and that would be a catastrophe, a deluge worse than the one in the bible. Bit by bit, our valiant efforts made us sweat a lot, and our fatigue brought us to a halt. Toward noon we were already half dead and the hole only reached our navels. After lunch we resumed our herculean task, and we dug like madmen until four o'clock, the fatal hour. That's when Madame Godin, who was looking for us everywhere, discovered us in our hole, next to the willow.

"What are you doing under my tree? Digging your grave, or what?"

Shamefaced as a beaten dog, Habéké explained that we wanted to go to China by the most direct way possible to solve a mystery, my mystery, that of my almond eyes, but Madame Godin called her husband to the rescue. Monsieur Godin arrived in a flash, crying out that he would kill us if we didn't immediately put all the earth back where it belonged, and it took us until nightfall to fill the hole again, at which point we were faced with a curious phenomenon: a surplus of earth, as if the hole had not been properly emptied, and we had to shovel what was left over into the river, fouling it up.

Later that night, having turned out the light, Habéké came in to lift my spirits.

"Anyway," he said, "I miscalculated the earth's diameter. According to my new calculations, we would have had to dig for three hundred thousand days, or eight hundred and twenty-one years..."

That enormity comforted me somewhat, and I slept well.

Eight

THREE HUNDRED AND FIFTEEN... three hundred and fourteen... three hundred and thirteen...

I had decided to count the telephone poles separating me from my semi-dwelling. There were four hundred and eighty-two, I knew it from a reliable source, Habéké, who counted them in sadness on his trips home.

Two hundred and sixty-five... two hundred and sixty-four... two hundred and sixty-three...

I let my eyes roam as night fell that Sunday before our saddened eyes, extinguishing the created world. Lights glimmered at the backs of fields, like a frontier of distant little brush fires, and I would have liked to fly off to those bushes; or were they like lanterns for a dragon festival beckoning me to the land of China, though we hadn't had enough time to make that happen.

Two hundred and eleven... two hundred and ten... two hundred and nine...

It was while scanning the oversized fields of those who knew nothing of hunger, and on thinking about my half of the planet, that I saw in dreams the third world and its realms of dust. In my dreams there came back to me the story Habéké had told me by the river, my friend talking freely, as he would in Africa where everything is transmitted mouth to mouth thanks to the old ones who know the myths and legends and who relate them at every opportunity, passing on knowledge and spawning worlds. Those tale tellers, the living books of the illiterate, are griots.

That morning Habéké had told me the story of a thin woman with many children, scraping out a living on arid land. Each year this woman sows her desert, hoping for a harvest, but nothing comes out of the earth, despite her suffering and her tears. One spring she decides to seed her world without pausing, day and night, with an energy born of desperation, and at the end of her strength she loses all her fingernails, which fall upon the earth. But she is too depleted to suffer, and under the pitiless sun she dies in front of her children. The hours pass like vultures turning in the burning sky, but the day after her death the children find ten green shoots pushing up through the crusted earth, ten little bushy heads born of ten nails sown by the deceased mother. The news spreads like wildfire toward all horizons, and people come running from afar to witness the extraordinary event. Across the land, no one has ever seen such fabulous bushes, which instead of leaves have human hands teeming with branches, hundreds of authentic little hands with fingers turned toward the sun, begging for a storm. The next day a miraculous rain falls for the first time in ages, and red fruits burst from the fingertips on every hand; fruits growing from succulent fingers. Soon after, the children harvest these mystical fruits, which prove to be their salvation, and so it is that the dead mother becomes the totem of an entire people imbued with her memory.

One hundred and sixty-one... a hundred and sixty... a hundred and fifty-nine...

I drowsed while obsessing over generations, and I saw a new world being born, far from the Accident and the adult era, and I was with Habéké, and we had children of our own. We would die for them, knowing that we were not the last word in the cosmic whirl of insignificant things, and those children would transform us into totems.

My head elsewhere, I fell asleep on my side of the seat, my hot forehead against the cool windowpane.

*

SUDDENLY, a friendly voice in the night.

"Hugues, we're here..."

I opened my eyes and found myself staring at my semi-home's front door. Already Monsieur Godin was opening the trunk to hand me my little bastard's bag, and I was all confused.

"Goodnight, my boy," said Madame Godin, who no longer seemed to resent me for being a boy. "You'll come back to see us. And send our greetings to your parents."

I mumbled "Yes, yes, good night, good night, thank you very much," then I gave Habéké a meaningful, manly look, the one that says "see you soon" and not farewell. In my bag, tucked into my Gustave Désuet book, there brightly burned the Geneva Convention that had warmed my heart ever since that night, and which reminded me that with Habéké I was less alone than ordinary mortals.

The headlights swept aside a thin mist, just substantial enough to veil a heart, and the station wagon was swallowed up in the darkness, slipping into a world bereft of color. Oh, little griot, I thought, oh Habéké of all my Africas, I wish you good night.

*

ALONE ON THE SIDEWALK, under the streetlight, I was not much more than a shadow. Pricking up my ears, I was surprised to hear muffled laughter and voices emanating from behind the house. I shoved my bag into the hedge to unburden myself, and I crept into the garden where, crouching down amid the prickly branches of our blue spruce, I could see without being seen. In the kitchen window's wide rectangle of light I saw my semi-parents, Céline with her hair down and Claude a bit tipsy, their voices loud, as were those of the uncles and aunts around a table littered with glasses of Coca-Cola and bottles of beer. They were spending the evening playing cribbage and telling dumb stories, while stealing glances at their neighbors' hands. They were smoking like chimneys, drinking and stuffing themselves, spluttering food right and left, shouting, betting and cheating, cursing, and carrying on like boors. I couldn't help thinking that they knew about my private secret, that they must be dishing out lots of dirt behind my back, saying: hey, Hugues, the bastard, doesn't he have the same eyes as the big Mohawk who lives over the grocery store; or the cook in the Chinese restaurant; or maybe what's his name, the Mongol who panhandles in front of the bank?

Suddenly Céline got up to open the back door and there was Pipo in person, my semi-pooch come to take the air, and who, with his merry snout, smelled me out in my prickly hiding place, welcoming me like a little dog who's been bored stiff. Oh Pipo, I'd been thinking of you, oh my little son of a bitch who understands me, and whom I understand so well, you missed me just as I missed you. When I got down on my knees to pet him he bathed my face in fraternal drool. A dog knows how to love, he slavers lovingly, as we would like people to do, but people would rather dribble malice, it's easier and more fun, and I decided that Pipo was perhaps the last kind heart in this family, which, after my two weeks of absence, struck me as a clan of barbarians. I realized that I no longer wanted to share the lives of these people, in this house where I stood for misgivings and impurity, where the foreignness of all other races was palpable in my own eyes. I had changed. I was dying to exit this finite world where everywhere there reigned, in the furtive depths of hard cold hearts, hypocrisy and the adult era. Monsieur and Madame Godin themselves were dying of cold, having never known who Habéké really was, having no idea of the fevered feelings hidden within him, because they labored body and soul to turn him into a sanitized man like all others, whereas Habéké himself was incomparable and without equal. Oh, they all dared to slyly smile, like the uncles and aunts sniggering in their stuffy little circles on my despairing Sundays after Mass, but who, back home, behind their living room curtains, rolled their revolted eyes, eyeing the blacks popping up in their neighborhoods, the wops, the polacks and the chinks who lowered the value of the nearby houses, once so hygienic and affluent, but today gangrened to the bone. Should you say "a black is drowning" or "a negro's gone under?"—Don't know.—Best not to say anything, just let him croak, ha! ha! You know what he's good for, an Italian stretched out on the grass?—Don't know.—Fertilizer, ha! ha! You know why the Chinese are yellow?—Don't know.—Because they piss against the wind, ha! ha! ha! Meanwhile they're bouncing their behinds on their chairs, but their grimaces signal their desire to sanitize everything and oppress everything, to wean us from the only sun I've ever loved, where all the gods' faces are molten, bathed in fire, the Ityopia that lovingly ravaged Habéké's bronzed visage, Habéké, my daytime star that blinded Claude and Céline, who from weakness or spite always denied my birth's inmost truth. My blood couldn't match the blood of their dreams, my blood did not flow in their veins. Well, I had news for them: we were going to purify ourselves all by ourselves, and I would in the end find the one I was, somewhere, in secret, because I existed elsewhere for a long time and it was always the same island I saw aloft in Exile's warm light, as I was awaiting myself, sitting under a tree, like a memory that had gone before me on the walkway of days, but I had split myself in two to mislead unbelievers.

Great gods, I had nothing to laugh about, and I begged Pipo to say nothing, to leave me to my follies, and above all not to follow me into the night. With that, I grabbed a stone lying at my feet and heaved it at the big kitchen window, which exploded in a crystalline din, then I made off through the hedge to lose myself far away, among the receding railroad lines.

I crossed through the industrial no man's lands where rail lines in marshalling yards were thick on the ground, and I wandered past the old rail cars. Swarms of anxious stars stared down on this cold, metallic world, and I remembered that when I was little I thought the sky was all made of sheet metal, like a gigantic sphere that took in the moon, sun, and stars, and that the only way to unearth the secret of life in the universe, the only possible way to lift a corner of the veil covering God's face, would be for a man to hoist himself to the sky's summit and cut a hole in the metal, pass his head through, and find the devil knows what, a thousand blinding truths, or perhaps one sole truth, but the real one, the greatest, the Key. But who could ever come to know those fabulous firmaments circling over the visible sphere? No one, I told myself, never anyone.

In the sky, without seeing them, I heard the creaking of bats, and in the darkness, without hearing them, I saw sparks shimmering, the fireflies of the fields that attended me like lucky charms. In my nebulous flight I began to dream of Habéké's Africa, my friend's world that so often eluded him so near to his truth. I saw myself fleeing with him already into the high plateaus of Ityopia, but something barred my way: the resumption of classes two days hence, the sad Tuesday following Labor Day, and I wanted to vomit up that school, that domain of the rich and strong that bleeds dry the poor and the weak, costs them their souls and inflicts endless suffering on the weak and poor, defenseless targets for the slavering strangler latent in the race of wolves—because yes, for the wolf, the wolf is a man.

I could remember still the soft flesh of one of our friends, Éric, who was overweight, but who was a prince of a man. Given his size and his debilitating slowness, Éric was a choice morsel for the cannibals. I recalled the morning in May at the bus stop where we were picked up, when a handful of imbeciles, a disgusting band of nobodies (the same who ate Habéké alive and attacked immigrants as a whole), forced Éric, on pain of death, to wallow in the mud and squeal like a pig. But Éric, from that point on, would no longer be anyone's enemy, nor, unfortunately their friend, as he left us for somewhere kept secret by his family, so that the curse would not follow them and hound them beyond time and space, but Éric and his parents lived in the clouds, because it was not a simple matter of fate, but rather a grave inhuman urge, and Éric would find no peace: the heartless everywhere spat upon minorities of his kind, and what wounded him would wound me forever, whatever the distance and the passing of time, because when one man suffers it's as if all suffer, beyond the women and children who come first.

The moon was now low, it was dipping toward the horizon like a disheartened soul. My fatigue weighed on me and I stretched out on a rail tie, amid an odor of tar, to rest a little, my head on a rail and my two legs on its parallel partner. All around, in the puddles, unseen toads were emitting comical burps, and I saw in the distance, between the rails, the moon shining like the bright eye of a locomotive. We don't really know who people are, I said to myself beneath the stars. They enjoy themselves because they have full bellies, but take the meat off their tables and they'll start slaughtering each other like wild animals. Every people, if left to its own devices, would exterminate all the other peoples vexing it or for which it has no need, that's human, and it's a universal dream. In the end, I said to myself, the Nazis were like someone you might meet anywhere, like Céline and Claude who would perhaps have enjoyed Jews being burned, or like the Godins perhaps, and my uncles and aunts as well, who knows?

That is when I had a vision.

I don't know if I was mad at that moment, or if I was a plaything of my imagination, but I saw a human form at the core of the moon's distant eye, a silhouette walking on the rail line. I was so fearful that I thought I was about to die, but I had enough strength left in me to flee.

*

SHORT OF BREATH but back again on my street under the trees, I pulled my bag out from the hedge, still frightened by what I had seen, and then I saw the police car.

When I stepped into my semi-home, I saw Pipo who was pulling in his muzzle and looking up at me from below, then I saw Claude, who was talking to a pair of policemen, then Céline in the kitchen with her broom and dustpan, cleaning up what was left of the shards of glass.

I was told that some thugs had shattered the big kitchen window and I tried to look appalled, but I was a welcome arrival to this ruined evening. My presence seemed to distract the guests scandalized by the waves of vandalism sweeping though our poor city, which had changed so radically since the influx of all those strange people rife with bad ideas and absurd beliefs.

That night, in bed, I thought about Africa and the scorpions aswarm under the stones. The large brown scorpions, Habéké had explained to me, are varieties of terrestrial crayfish that are not life threatening, but it's the little black scorpions that harbor in their tails' last ring a deposit of poison, their own brand of nastiness. But what is hardest to understand is that the black scorpions, despite their powers, are cowards to the core. Habéké had explained to me that such a scorpion, imprisoned by a ring of flames, would inject itself and kill itself rather than face up to the danger and die like a man. I thought that this was surely the same syndrome shared by the aunts, uncles, and everyone around, including Claude and Céline, who would doubtless choose to end their lives rather than face up to my truths.

I could have set fire to the house to see which of my alleged kin, those little black scorpions, would kill themselves rather than confront my fire. It would have been a good way to put faces onto traitorous, decapitated bodies, but then I fell asleep.

Nine

A STRANGE SUN, ill and milky, emptied of its summer light, translucid as a thumbnail, had opened its weary eye on the first morning of this school year that dispirited me so, I who dreamed of Africas with their pathways of fire and our island of Exile. Alas, I was living deep underground, where no light, no truth, could reach me. I felt that I was no longer the body bearing my name and owning my eyes, but rather a sad and faceless shadow dogging its steps. I must leave, I said to myself, I must go far from here, far from these nights, to where we will build ourselves a world free of the Accident, yet unseen forces held me fast inside this life, with restraints I could not fathom, and though I wanted to tear everything down, to go off and be reborn on the far side of things, my legs would not carry me, and I did not yet have the strength to embrace my freedom.

While I was pining in my room, Jasmine and Benjamin were loving the world just as it was reflected in their shiny shoes, but they can be forgiven for all that: their crime is called innocence, and all they wanted was to one day become something; Benjamin, an Egyptologist, and Jasmine, a veterinariette.

"Yes, veterinariette. We say major and majorette, star and starlet, quart and quartet..."

Not bad, Jasmine, Benjamin too; they were a pair of little loves who did honor to their parents. They would be the pride and joy of their holy family!

Still, the little dolled up darlings scurried from here to there in the house, seeking a pencil box, a slipper, a barrette, with Pipo barking for no reason, all of which put me in a bad mood.

That morning, at the bus stop, I felt somewhat happy all the same, meeting the friends unseen all summer, tanned and taller, like me, I imagine. Habéké was there, his school-bag strapped on, his legs protruding beyond his attractive Bermudas, long legs topped by a short-sleeved shirt that lent him a certain elegance. All scrubbed and lovely, he smelled of soap, but no longer wore magic bracelets on his wrist, nor his cornelian necklace at his throat. His parents now forbade him from donning those ornaments to go to school, but he hailed me with a smile: "Hello, you!" I replied, "Hello, my blackie!", and we gave each other friendly taps on the shoulder, our eyes brimming with secrets and dreams that were ours alone.

Sitting on the water fountain, Bruno Jolicoeur, the guy whose chin was like baby buttocks, had already started to shower us with the jokes and obscenities he'd garnered from his uncles over the summer around their barbecues and swimming pools, and he had the memory of an elephant, did Bruno, there was no way to mute the gramophone.

"What's the difference between a car and a woman?"

We didn't know.

"A car has headlights and a woman's light in the head."

No one laughed at his joke and the girls treated him like an idiot, which is no surprise given the sensitivity of the female sex. Then the tall Marie-France Bastien arrived with her left arm in a cast, the arm she didn't write with.

"I fell on a rock while I was water skiing, but it could have been worse, like my cousin said, I could have broken a ski."

Meanwhile, Benoit appeared with a swollen lip, all stitched up, and a face covered in scratches; but he also brought us the incredible story of a seaplane accident in Timiskaming, with his godfather hanging on to the joystick. He told the tale of his misadventure so well that we formed a circle around him, hanging onto his words, wanting to know how the episode turned out. We lapped up his account of this miracle, and it was as if we'd been there when the plane struck the electric wires and nose-dived into Lake Cawasachouane, where everyone had been fished out by Algonquins passing by in a canoe.

"Lucky you!" exclaimed Alexandre, who was envious of Benoît's daredevil godfather, his wonderful seaplane accident, and all his eye-catching wounds that were a source of fascination to the girls. "Why doesn't that ever happen to me, things like that?"

Whereupon Bruno the clown came up with another bad joke.

"You know about the guy with five penises?"

We all shrugged our shoulders at the same time.

"No? Well let me tell you, his underpants fit him like a glove!"

This time we laughed, especially the boys who were well aware of the girls going red in the face with disapproval. He was dumb as an ox, Bruno Jolicoeur, but we were making him happy.

Next to the mailbox there was one guy not laughing at that barbecuers' gag. It was Jérome, who had a mother who was a man. It seems that the woman's deficiency was caused by a serious hormonal identity crisis and the surgeons had fashioned for Jérome's mother a sort of penis with flesh but no bone, using muscle parts taken from elsewhere plus soft tissue reinjected under the skin to wrap around the organ and give it an appearance pleasant to the naked eye, with a shape and size that seemed appropriate. Since then Jérome's mother had changed radically, both in her body and in her migrant soul. She lived near Shawinigan, now with a wife to please, seeking a new version of harmony and bliss. Meanwhile Jérome's real father, in his gloom, and under the misapprehension that he might once again win over his former spouse, was thinking of offering his body to science for an experiment that would involve grafting an embryo onto his not very appropriate abdomen, a curious idea inspired by seahorses, whose males do lend themselves to gestation.

Meanwhile, some of the older students from the high school were drawing near us. When there were enough of them to give themselves the backbone, they decided to give us a hard time. One of the first brayed:

"Hey! Béké whatever! I saw you this summer at the Granby Zoo!"

I clenched my teeth just like Habéké because this was something we weren't used to. A moment later, another student shouted:

"Me, I saw your whole family at the Safari Preserve. They were eating bananas in a tree!"

Defenseless now, Habéké turned around, his heart broken. His back was to me, but I could see his hands shaking, as if he were dreaming of strangling someone.

"Hey! The Chink!"

This time I was the target.

"Hey! The Mongol! Did you eat your stinking dog this summer?"

Just then the yellow bus turned the corner and stopped

next to us in a cloud of dust. We followed the cretins on board, all of whom went to sit at the back to wallow in their filth. I went to sit with Habéké, who was still out of sorts.

Just as the bus was about to leave, we saw a girl with long black hair running into the middle of the street.

"Hey! Wait, mister," cried Marie-France Bastien, "there's a girl coming!"

The driver reopened the door, and that's how Odile came into our lives looming large right before our eyes, Odile and her big, beautiful capital O, as in: "O Odile of my silence and my secret self." But we didn't yet know what she would be for us. The first time we saw her she was just a newcomer who'd turned up over the summer while our backs were turned, hatched secretly in a hidden garden, a girl of gestures and splendors; but not so much a girl as a breath of air who rendered me all confused and stupid, a lucky charm with a raspberry mouth and porcelain teeth, the cheekbones of a shameless little pest and beautiful big lamb's eyes set off by a milky complexion. I could sense a heart of gold beating all through to the tips of her lashes, and my own heart was pounding all the way to my fingertips when she slid onto the seat in front of us next to Marie-France in her cast.

"Ouf! I didn't know where the stop was!"

I looked at Habéké, who saw me looking at him, and our eyes, on meeting, greeted each other like old friends. So I leaned forward a little and mumbled whatever came into my mind.

"Hi... uh... you're called what?"

"What? What the heck and whaddya know!"

The two girls burst out laughing and Habéké shot me an angry look, but I'd tried my best.

"And you," asked the newbie, "are you called Why?"

"No, he's called the Chinaman," said Marie-France.

"But he's not Chinese," remarked the new girl.

"No, but he's called that because of his slanted eyes, and his friend sitting beside him is called Oo, Oo Becky Oo Ksoom!"

Habéké and I got the message, and we buried ourselves up to our ears in the seat, but at least, I said to myself, given this mess we were in together, Habéké had forgotten about the big boors parked at the back of the bus.

"Don't get all uptight, boys" Marie-France sniped over the back of her seat, her face distorted by the sadistic delight she was taking in breaking our hearts. "She'll never be in your class, she's too old, too bad, you should have come into the world on time, lazy birds!"

*

It was only later, on the way home, that the newbie agreed to talk to us normally. We learned that she lived on rue Lanthier, beyond the arena, in what used to be our friend Éric's house, himself now somewhere under other unkind skies.

"I was new too, last year," said Habéké, "I had it hard, but now I'm not so new, and sometimes they just forget about me."

The truth was that Habéké still had it pretty hard, but I didn't want to twist the knife in his wound.

"Anyway, I'm Habéké Axoum."

"And my name is Hugues."

"Fugue?"

"Hugues. With an "h.""

I thought she liked us okay, even if we were nervous.

"I'm Odile."

We shook her velvety hand with its lovely pearly nails that reminded me of the oyster shells at the chalet.

"Does that mean they're going to laugh at me a lot?"

"I don't think so," I reassured her, "I wouldn't worry about it. You're lucky to be a girl and girls aren't like everybody else because of maternal love."

"Ah..."

"But especially," said Habéké, "you're not black and that will help you to pass unnoticed, because I guess that's what you want."

"Um... I guess so, yes..."

She wasn't sure about anything.

"Me," said Habéké, "that's been my dream for a long time, to pass unnoticed, like Éric who stayed where you're staying, but it seems like people who always pass unnoticed aren't any happier, so why cry about it? You have to be hard as a rock..."

Poor Odile looked puzzled, and I tried to come to her rescue.

"Habéké's talking about the soul, yes, the soul's hard rock that has you staying the way you are, like a king inside yourself."

"Like a negus," Habéké corrected me.

"What are you talking about?" Odile exclaimed. "I don't understand a thing you're saying!"

"We're talking about being well born," I replied, "of a mother who's rich emotionally and has a determining factor, like Gustave Désuet says."

"Who? Gustave who? One of your friends?"

"No, the poet who we always have at lunch, who we love like a brother and who died young, but just a minute..."

At that, I opened my lunch box to show her that we weren't making fun of her, but she'd made up her mind and went to sit farther on, not with just anyone, but with the handsome Alexandre, who was her age and shared her style.

"She has pizzazz, that little imp with the nice eyes..."

Stunned to see her seeking refuge next to a rival, I held Gustave's book stupidly on my knees. I opened it anyway at random, just to take a look before putting it back in my lunch box, and I happened on a poem that I'd read it a hundred times.

Oh my sorry life! Oh my desolation!

I flee my ailing body
on this fateful day born into cries
where History knows no hope,
but is fatality regained,
and so my fire, my home, my soul are all extinguished.

Oh evil flame! Oh inward rage!

I will have seen that the sex of a woman
is a dream
wherein dying one meets the child that he was,
the mother who bore him,
and all the centuries' suffering reduced to the sex of
    a man,
the lachrymose sex of his father.

Oh mercy mine! Oh the anguish of men!

In death they bear off
all the evil they have done
with the greedy gland
of their maddened rod
crowned head of their monotheism.

We didn't understand the poem very well, but we loved the words that descended, it seemed to us, like water drops into a torture chamber. One day, we told ourselves, one fine day, we would understand, that was certain, and we couldn't wait.

*

GIVEN THAT HABÉKÉ and I found ourselves seated alone under circumstances conducive to confession, I decided to talk about the vision I saw on the railroad line.

"Listen... you're going to think I'm sick or crazy, but... I think I saw him."

"What? What did you see?"

"On Sunday, the day you left me off in front of our house, I didn't go in right away. Instead I went walking on the rail line where you often go running at night, in the moonlight, and I saw a silhouette, a shadow walking like a ghost, perhaps the wandering ghost of your great-grandfather..."

I'd been afraid of talking to Habéké, of telling him the truth about my specter, because of the shock such revelations can have, and I was still wondering whether I was dreaming back there in the lunar night, but finally I told him what I'd seen, and Habéké seemed to slump beside me, stunned and amazed, and he said nothing more during the trip. I saw our town's small houses gliding past the bus's windows like islands detached from their setting, swept along by the passing of time behind Habéké's inky face, his nocturnal silhouette fronting the day's glaring backdrop; meanwhile Odile was there before us laughing beside Alexandre, I saw their lips moving but I didn't know what they were saying, I was suddenly deaf and it was as if I were in the midst of a dream. I basked in this translucence, the translucence of a world where we feel ourselves at times to be no more than a veil belonging to no one, and that night in the bus, surrounded my nebulous fellows and beside Habéké whose shoulder rubbed against mine, for one blinding moment I saw myself growing old.

Ten

EVERY NIGHT during the first weeks of school, when I found myself between the covers, I saw Odile gliding over me in her golden glow, and I realized that I had never dared associate a girl with this sky-high radiance, I had never seen in a girl what I now saw in the dimness of my room, and despite the fact that she was a bit older than Habéké and me, the gap was not huge, meaning she glimmered just beyond our fingertips, still in the realm of the possible, where our hopes end but where life begins. Odile was a rare, hallowed realm that we might hope to attain. And too, while she was not yet a woman in full bloom, she radiated a completeness and the consecrated mystery that girls of our age had not yet displayed, or at least that I had never perceived. When I saw Odile in the flesh, in the street, on the bus, or at school, I could picture her supernatural physical incarnations, as if my maturing gaze had infiltrated her clothing and my eyes were passing like clouds over her skin; but that discomfited me greatly and I blushed from seeing so much, as never before had I dared to venture so deeply into a girl, not even into women who were fully formed and perfect, I mean married or engaged women who are complete, nor even among the naked and spreadeagled women in magazines, as if in the veneer of women who were too naked I no longer saw their nudity and I was bored, as if I could no longer sense the invisible I longed for, or as if this nakedness was uninhabited and my gaze passed lifelessly through it without there being any core to what was there, or any density of soul, because what I sought in nudity's essence was the world and its pulsations, and not to exalt myself, what I sought was life, and that's why Odile's hidden nudity scorched my eyes, because the world as a whole was nestled there, contained in her and her thoughts, her pith and her substance, her tremors and her flame, and what I saw troubled me immensely, as when at mass, as a child, I truly saw Christ in the host, saw the holy ghost where the church soared heavenwards, but at the same time my heart was learning to live thanks to this adoration, and I felt a warmth coming alive for her in the crooks of my arms and as far off as my fingertips and my lips; and in my madness I thought I had perhaps been visited by something resembling love, yet I couldn't know for sure, given my age and emotional immaturity. And when at night I imagined myself caressing Odile, I was someone charming whom I had not yet known, and I was so possessed that it frightened me, because perhaps I was sick or mad, and at night I saw Odile stretched out in my bed, up against me, so close that her breath misted my cheek with delicate droplets of herself, and in my dream it was all so simple that I was happy.

Those nights, I was so troubled that I phoned Habéké at impossible hours and I persuaded Madame Godin to go and get him out of bed because it was urgent. At last I heard his sleepy voice, the voice of my friend who put my heart back in its place.

"Hello, Habéké... I'm sick..."

I told him what I'd seen in my bedroom's darkness, all the visions that had come over me. Habéké listened in silence, but I know he saw totems turning in circles in his own head's heaven, and he understood the majesty of Odile.

Eleven

FRIDAY NIGHT, after three weeks of school, as long as three eternities, Habéké and I, as one in our secrets and dreams, were at last ready to make the trip we'd promised each other, our journey to the deepest heart of Africa.

"Do you have the tent?"

"I have everything, except for a flashlight and the cans of stew."

To protect ourselves against the likelihood of lions, we had brought along a sort of armor: my goalie's gear. We'd lashed our baggage onto our sidecars, little wagons attached to our bicycles, which would go with us along the northern roads. We wondered what we would find beyond the horizon, but we still dared to believe in miracles, because a miracle, so it was said, is perhaps just a question of will. All it takes is an intense desire for it to occur; to wish for it forcefully so as to extricate it from the unseen world where it lingers amid everything one wishes for, to lure it into the light, and to make it truly exist the way everything else exists. And this miracle would perhaps be Africa, the real Africa, the one that smells of lamp oil, gunpowder, and the vanilla of coffee blossoms, with its flocks and its wells, its savannahs and its wild animals, its peoples, its spirits, and its tatagu kononi reincarnated in Mekkonen the dedjené, Habéké's great-grandfather.

That night, fully prepared for the dawning day, we wandered the streets, gazing searchingly at the people we passed in case we would never return from Ityopia's plateaus. As was to be expected we made a detour along rue Lanthier to where our pulsing hearts led us by the nose, to where we were spellbound by a house unlike the others, and to where the lit window of Odile's room was for us a fount of light.

"We could maybe go and knock on her door," Habéké said, "or scratch at her window to tell her we're thinking of her."

"I'm afraid to talk to her."

We stayed there for a long time, rooted like two plum trees on the brink of life, and then, having worshipped the light, we headed home, our hands empty and our hearts full.

*

I SLEPT POORLY that night, twisting about under my bedclothes like a lettuce worm, perturbed by nightmares that made no sense. I don't know what it was, a fear of dying perhaps, but on waking I felt a bit better because it was a new day with a beaming September sun caught by my curtains, warming my face at the corner of my pillow.

Everyone in the house was still sleeping when I took off on my Mustang bicycle. I left a note on the table that said that I was sleeping over at Habéké's that night, just as Habéké left one on his saying that he was sleeping at mine, but in fact we would be dreaming under the stars. So now I went to find Habéké, who was waiting for me in front of his house, butterflies in his stomach. We bucked each other up and pedaled first toward the rail line, but on the way we faltered and once again found ourselves on rue Lanthier, where we had the surprise of our life: Odile herself was outside! Sitting there with her long black hair splayed over her shoulders, she was keeping an eye on two children gamboling on the lawn. Lifting her chin, she saw us.

"Hey! What are you doing here?"

We stopped, even though our hearts were pounding.

"Hi," said Habéké, "How come you're up at this hour?"

"I'm watching Philippe and Marilou."

Clearly, they were her brother and sister. An elusive family resemblance played across their faces.

"What's in your sidecars?"

"Our baggage," Habéké replied.

"Are you going on a trip?"

We didn't want to disclose our secrets, it was too soon, but Odile began to circle our carriers, checking them out.

"Hey! Swords! You're taking swords!"

Yes, we were carrying two long wooden swords that I'd been storing in the basement for a long time, and that I'd brought out for our perilous crossing through an unknown world.

"Will you be meeting dragons?"

She could laugh as much as she liked, but we were very serious, yet how could we, in one meager human breath, convey a lifetime's accretion of secrets? Only poorly, that was obvious, but we had to try, and that is how, next to the sidewalk, on that Saturday morning when we were heading out for the high country, I told Odile the story of our births as accursed bastards, describing in sadness Habéké's catastrophic drought. I spoke of recurrent wars, a despairing refrain for mankind, of the terrible deaths Habéké had witnessed within his family, of the insect that drinks at night upon the dune and that once saved a child's life, of Habéké's being torn away from the land of his anguished bloodline, then of his coming ashore beyond the seas in the realm of the Accident, armed with Gustave Désuet's poems, our wanting to change the world, with a digression regarding the medical certificates without which Habéké could have just as easily succumbed like carrion in his ruined land, given that defective children in poor countries, in their cadaverous condition, weigh much less in the balance than the Accidentals' bank accounts, a good lesson for those little lepers, teaching them how not to exist when we look at them, which is a comfort for all concerned. Seeing that Odile was listening intently, I told her about my off-putting birth that had repelled persons unknown, my abandonment in a supermarket cart surrounded by bulrushes, my long eyes whose antecedents I would one day seek out in China; then I told her about the dream life we harbored within us just as you carry sleeping children. I disclosed our marriage in the bushes amid flames and vows of eternal fidelity, I explained the tatagu kononi and the sacred balanza, our totems, and then I told of our wish to sail off and populate the island of our beliefs, in exile, far from hypocrisy and the adult era. When I'd finished, Odile clutched the children to her and looked at us strangely.

Suddenly, Habéké broke the silence by asking politely whether Odile had a photograph of herself in case of emergency.

"I still don't understand where you're going."

"We're going to ride as far as we can toward the north," I said, "along the rail line that runs into the mountains where tonight we'll sleep in the forest. We don't know what we'll find there, but we hope to see signs of Habéké's great-grandfather."

Hearing these words, Odile turned her eyes toward Habéké, who said:

"Yes, I'm sure his living spirit is not far from here, I feel it, he's seeking me out to bring me back to the circle of my people, because for them my spirit has been held hostage by evil spirits, and they are unhappy in their deaths, down there, and have sent the ancestor Mekkonen to find me and calm my spirit, but as long as all those who are lost are not returned to their native skies by the dedjené, those who have survived and those born after me will have unhappy lives, difficult hunting, disastrous harvests, stillborn children, and sicknesses barking at their heels..."

After which, Habéké and I went silent, as we had said it all. We stood there watching Odile, who was watching us...

"Good," I said at last, "we'll be on our way..."

"Wait a minute," said Odile, and she left us with the children to go looking for something inside the house.

Little Philippe dared to open his mouth.

"Are you gon fight for real against mossers with swords?"

I said yes, and his face looked grave.

"Do you want to come with us?" I asked, just for fun. "We have room."

"No!" cried Marilou, "I want to stay with Odile!"

Just then Odile reappeared with a photo for Habéké.

"Bon voyage, guys! Take care!"

The children said goodbye, but we had a photograph as a harbinger of hopefulness and a melodious voice to bring us comfort.

*

WE SET OFF on the path that ran alongside the rail line. After having crossed through the wasteland, we found ourselves in the industrial zone, in the marshalling yards where the Canadian National railcars were rusting away.

"It's near here where I saw the ghost, that other time..."

Along our way we were met with catcalls from drivers at level crossings, and people astounded to see us passing through the no man's lands on their dusty roads. At last we exited the city through a keyhole, a short tunnel under the highway, bound for vastness.

Farther on, the rail line entered a forest, and the incline made us work, so we stopped to drink from our bottles, and I saw Habéké first pouring a bit of water onto the stony ground.

We were entering the unknown, we'd soon be on the plateaus. We felt as if we were acceding to the truth.

"We have to keep our eyes open."

"Yes, each of us one eye."

"Watch for smoke between the trees, that could very well be my great-grandfather."

There was no one left in the vicinity, where already we heard the cries of wildlife, but we took deep breaths and climbed onto our bicycles. We began to ride slowly through the high grasses, where clouds of grasshoppers were flying off in all directions. Habéké shouted to me that this was perhaps a sign that we were already nearing Africa, where at times, it seems, the trees are so full of locusts that you're constantly showered with tiny droppings. Then we pedaled faster and faster along the path following the rail line, eyes wide open on this world that more and more was swallowing us up and bewitching us.

All afternoon we pedaled like mad, seeking the Ityopya of our dreams and Mekkonen the dedjené, the ancestral spirit dispatched to the underside of our skies by the distant, restless dead. Soon, without realizing it, we were no longer in the land we knew, but were rolling through Abyssinia's blue mountains, through spiny brush where shadows stirred, where silhouettes were in hiding behind the trunks of dead trees. Often the rail line crossed clay ravines where there ran a yellow stream or the discharge from a lake where we saw beaver huts, or perhaps they were giant termitaria or volcanic hillocks, we no longer knew what we saw. Then we crossed through dense woods and rocky meadows where hawthorns grew, looking like locust trees Habéké said, or like sumacs where they'd cut down trees, umbrella-like mimosas or aspens, eucalyptuses, elms, hackberries, big thuyas leaning out over the sandy river, enormous kapok trees or tufted bulrushes, aloes. That heron down in the pond was perhaps a witch doctor; those goldfinches in the bluegrass, flights of weaverbirds; this rock in the river, a hippopotamus; and the dark holes doubtless hid lions, hyenas, and monkeys.

At one point we stopped at the edge of a burn field to pick blueberries, but Habéké let out a cry, and we fled on our bicycles. My friend had spotted at the edge of the forest a tall warrior, solitary and forbidding, brandishing an ox horn full of beer and a cow tail to chase off tsetse flies—perhaps it was just a charred stump, but perhaps not, and we had done well to take to our heels.

Around noon, when we'd stopped to eat, we pricked up our ears, listening for movement in the forest. At the merest snap, Habéké jumped up and cried: "Mekkonen! Dedjené! Mekkonen!" Sitting in the hay near a stream, I let my friend call out as much as he wished. Finally, when he rejoined me, we ate sardines and hard-boiled eggs without exchanging words, seen that we were deeply immersed in Ityopya, and I told myself that I strongly believed in it, in the spirits that are little gods full of feeling that twirl about in the atmosphere, together with thoughts and presences. In sidelong glances I eyed Habéké, admiring his long black fingers with their pale nails fishing out oily sardines shaped into cockscombs from the bottom of the tin. As was his way with all food and drink, Habéké sacrificed a portion, the first sardine that he lobbed far off into the grass, because it was "part of the earth." I then observed his eyes, always on the alert, and saw, past his nose, his lovely head permeated with religion. I remembered that we had already quarreled about church, which I no longer attended on Sundays despite the admonitions of my semi-parents. Habéké had reproached me for no longer believing. He said that if you abused the Bible the way Gustave Désuet did in his poems, you could not hurt the gods, because the Bible is just an object written by a few men, while the gods in their multitude are the salvation of all and sundry, they are the infinite's very breath that inhabits the realm of dreams and as such are untouchable, and life has no meaning without gods, as water has no meaning without a man and his thirst. To end with a flourish Habéké silenced me with his African parable about the young rich man and the old poor man.

> *The old man who has nothing,*
> *what you say is not loved;*
> *you are in the right,*
> *but people don't like what you say.*

> *The rich young man,*
> *people like what you say,*
> *what you say is not true,*
> *but we like what you say.*

"To speak badly of the gods is fashionable, and I think you are speaking of the gods like a rich young man because you are following this fashion like a little white sheep, the same as all your fellows."

He had backed me into a corner, but since that famous quarrel, lo and behold I began to believe in Habéké's spirits, in the legion of free souls abroad in the indistinctness that surrounds us all throughout our lives, and I truly thought that, on this Saturday at the end of September, I would not be surprised to suddenly see, at a bend in the rail line, not only Mekkonen the dedjené, but my own great-grandfather as well, my unknown ancestor seeking my lost spirit so as to rescue it from forces of evil.

I reflected on all that, on faith and gods, on spirits and men, when all of a sudden I had an urge to see in order to believe.

"Can you show me Odile's picture?"

Habéké wiped his hands on the spears of couch grass and pulled from his pocket our friend's little photograph.

"You can keep it on you, if you want."

I would keep it on me, and how! And not just on me, over the heart in the middle of my chest, but within me, in a little chapel that would be home to this spirit's icon burning my fingers.

I carefully placed Odile's photo on a large dandelion so we could see it well, and so she could see us from deep in her life; this photo was a small window opening onto our world where our sky ran like water into her world, bearing our eyes to hers. Then I peeled a hardboiled egg after cracking it on my skull.

It was then that Habéké, who had seen what I had done, spoke to me about a man out of his distant African childhood, Sissaye, a poor goatherd who kept his grandfather's skull in his hut to pray to that kind spirit and ask him to watch over his kids. One day, despite the goatherd's prayers and offerings, clouds covered the sky and it began to rain so hard that the torrents ravaged the land and swept away almost all the young goats. Sissaye threw himself into the middle of the deluge, searching for his animals, but after a week was back in the village, his hands empty and his feet bloodied. It was then that, entering his hut, Sissaye let out a scream: two intruders were ensconced in his grandfather's skull, two little birds that had made their nests in the dead man's open mouth and who'd laid an egg. Weeping from despair because his ancestor's soul was captive to the shell, Sissaye left his hut, a sword in his fist, disembowelled his last kid, and wrenched out its insides. Then he placed the steaming entrails over the egg so it would hatch, but the egg never did. A few days later a sorcerer danced and sang inside Sissaye's hut to try and trap the elder's spirit between his rod and his drumskin, but the spirit had been killed by his offenses and poor Sissaye threw the egg up into the mountain, where his grandfather's soul decomposed among the stones. And that is how the skull became mute, and Sissaye an orphan, which was a sin and a grave impurity. To punish himself Sissaye placed burning coals in his mouth and put out his eyes with acacia thorns.

After having told me this story, Habéké made a sacrifice of one of his two eggs and threw it far off, into a field.

"That's the spirits' share..."

*

WE PUSHED ON all afternoon with thousands of pedal strokes, making our way under the sun and through the wind that sometimes hit us hard, but we stayed the course, forging on to the heart of Africa. Habéké took the lead, and I found it hard to keep close to him. Fired up, he sped down the narrow path bristling with sharp grasses that scraped our thighs, our carriers bounding into the air, propelled by bumps or groundhog holes. We crossed wild fields, forests of spruce and clusters of birch, we crossed streams, and for a long time followed a lovely river whose water was red.

When we stopped at nightfall, Habéké didn't seem too tired, while I had my tongue hanging out. We eyed each other, sighing, sorry not to have detected any trace of the ancestor, then we unloaded our baggage to prepare our camp.

While I raised the tent on the sandy ground of a fir forest, Habéké gathered wood to make a fire. The wind was down, but we could see our breath and we knew the night would be cold. By the time we sat ourselves near the flames to keep ourselves warm, twilight was settling in, and the crackling fire shot sparks into the sky to seed the stars. We opened the cans of stew that we were going to heat over the coals, but we were so hungry that we started gobbling it down gulp after gulp.

We planted knives between our feet and thrust our swords into the sandy soil within easy reach of our hands, because we didn't feel safe: we heard all sorts of noises around us, as if wild animals were lurking in the shadows. Habéké sniffed out the night with all his ancient wisdom, seeking the scents of dead animals that follow in the wake of hyenas, but the smell of the stew frustrated his efforts.

Once the stew was boiling hot, we were finally able to devour it after offering a little to the earth. It felt so good to be eating something warm that we began to chat.

"I wonder at what age you can no longer die young, Habéké asked aloud between two spoonfuls of stew."

"Good question. I'd say at about twenty-nine."

"Ah? Why twenty-nine?"

"Because Gustave Désuet died at twenty-nine and they say in the books that he died young. Anyway, it seems to me that thirty is starting to be a bit old, no?"

"I don't think it's a matter of age. I mean some people could die young at eighty, but others have died old at the age of twenty."

That wasn't so dumb, what he had just said. I shoveled in a mouthful of stew, thinking about it a little, then I said:

"How would you like to die?"

"I don't know. It doesn't matter, but not of thirst. You?"

"Me, it doesn't matter, but not burned alive. Drowned, maybe. Seems it's a good death, that's what they say, anyway."

"And murdered, would you like that?"

"It depends by whom. If it's being killed by Odile out of love, that's fine, for her I'd spill my blood."

"If you were killed out of hatred by another man who loves Odile?"

"Oh no! That would be worse than being buried alive!"

That said, I brought Odile's photo out of my pocket to admire it in the light of the flames.

Suddenly, I asked Habéké a question that had been nagging at me since the very start.

"Do you absolutely want to marry a black woman?"

I don't know why, but he answered me with another question.

"And you?"

"Well, me, if it weren't for Odile, I'd be able to imagine myself with a black woman."

"And I'd be able to imagine myself with a white woman."

After that we waited a long time without talking, just staring at the coals. Our stomachs were full and our muscles relaxed, our faces aglow from the flames, like masks of the sun. We were fine, less afraid, perhaps because we had dared to talk man to man and that had reassured us.

The fire went out at last, and we saw more clearly the firs silhouetted against the starry sky, their lofty whisks tickling the Great Bear's belly, but the stillness was chilling our blood.

"It's starting to get cold," I said.

We got up, all bent over, then took our knives and our swords to go and lie down in the tent around which fireflies flew in circles. I remember the smell of the broad canvas and the smoke clinging to our clothes. I remember the chirping of the crickets and the music from a stream running by, not far off. I also remember the softness of the ground beneath the tent and the joy of stretching out on a bed of sand. I wondered whether we were far enough from home to be in exile. But I especially remember what Habéké murmured as we slid towards sleep.

"There are all sorts of signs... the cry of a jackal at night... and above all... of a chameleon on a red anthill..."

"What? What are you saying?"

"If you're there... if you're there when it happens to me... you must make me stand tall... under a balanza or a poplar tree... I mean in the earth... standing... and above all.... above all you'll have to tie a strip of white cotton to a branch... because that's the symbol... the symbol of the word belonging to whoever has gone on..."

*

MY EYE HALF OPEN over my tattered dreams, I saw the pale morning beyond the tent, and I heard the amazing cawing of the crows, but I turned about to wriggle my behind and burrow myself in the sand, so I might go back to sleep and have a lazy dawn.

"Can you hear the crows?" Habéké asked me.

"You're not sleeping?"

"I'm awake..."

A half hour later the sun showed itself between the firs' branchlets and shone with all its ardor through the canvas. We decided to get up and, exiting the tent, were filled with wonder at the sight of dew coating the ground with a glistening veil.

"Did you hear the train going by last night?"

"Yes, it was heading north."

While Habéké pulled out the stakes and folded the tent, I set myself to relighting the fire in the ring of stones. Squatting, I was astonished that nothing in the woods was in movement, no breath of wind was stirring the branches, yet there were still the cursed crows shouting themselves hoarse higher up on the train line.

"I'd love to know what's going on," said Habéké.

"Okay, let's go."

As soon as we set foot on the rails, we saw, a hundred yards distant, dozens of crows wheeling and squealing over the landscape.

"You'd think there was something there, in the bushes."

"I'm sure there are hyenas, I can feel it!"

Habéké sniffed the air, sought tracks in the sand, and I felt a resurgence of fear, sensing an Africa, like a lesion, coming back to life.

"I'm afraid! I'm going to put on my goalie's gear!"

We went back to the camp where Habéké helped me to strap on my leather leggings, the pad, the mitt, and the mask, and that's how, in my hockey armor, I set off, clutching my sword, creeping step by step over the rail ties, wary of leopards and lions.

A few steps short of this strange phenomenon, the crows came close to attacking us. My legs were like jelly and my stomach was churning. I sighed deeply and took off my mask.

"Here," I said, turning toward Habéké, "at least put on my goalie's mask."

With that, I left the rails to go a short way into the woods. I spread out the branches with my sword and I felt Habéké on my heels, pressed up against me. Suddenly, entering a clearing below the crows' funnel, I saw what I never would have wanted to see and felt blood surging into my chest, but a memory lapse has blotted out my flight. The first thing I recall is the camp where I am on the ground, tangled up in my leg pads and suffocating in my chest protector, with Habéké, pale, beside me (yes, Habéké pale). Just looking into his eyes, I knew that he too saw the bones in the undergrowth.

"Did you see that?" he kept asking me, "Did you see the bones?"

"Yes... I saw them... but what kind of bones are they, do you think?"

"Human bones!"

"Are you sure?"

"You didn't see the skull?"

"There was a skull?"

"Yes, a broken skull, my great-grandfather's skull, I'm sure, because my great-grandfather was a broken man..."

His eyes brimming with tears, Habéké began to moan, thinking about his Africa dead in the bushes, then he took off running toward the bones.

"Habéké! Don't go back there!"

I was shouting myself hoarse, but my friend ignored me. I yanked off my goalie's gear, and by the time I got back to the rail line Habéké was speeding my way with a long bone and part of a skull—they may have been just fragments of a moose or of a bear rotting in the foliage, but perhaps they really were the human remains of Mekkonen the magician, in any case Habéké was certain of it and he convinced me.

"Quick! Let's get out of here!"

We jumped on our bicycles and took off, leaving everything behind, the tent, the swords, the leg pads, everything, heads down we tore toward the house, so fast that at one point the rope snapped behind me and my carrier tumbled down a steep slope like a ton of bricks. I didn't even take the time to stop for it.

We pedaled all morning, stopping just once to drink at a stream. As it was pretty well all downhill, we burned up the path, and at about two o'clock passed through the tunnel under the highway to come out into the industrial zone.

It was when we reached the streets that I saw that I was riding jerkily, that my front tire was flat.

After having annihilated all of Africa that we had created the day before, we ended up at the Kik-Cola grocery store, facing the arena, where we collapsed onto the steps to catch our breath. We looked at each other and were so exhausted that we could hardly speak.

"Stay here," I said at last, "I'll go and buy something to eat."

When I came out of the store with cakes and some cartons of milk, Habéké was clutching the backpack in which he had brought back the bones, and I saw the despair in his eyes. Poor Habéké, I thought to myself, poor guy, who has done so much, searching for Mekkonen the dedjené through all the Ityopyas in his most beautiful dreams, but who has been left with only the remnants of a man.

*

THE NEXT DAY, to my great distress, Habéké was missing from class. In the school bus I described our mishaps to Odile, who couldn't believe her ears, and who reacted negatively to Habéké's behavior.

That day I couldn't take in anything our teachers said. After school I phoned Habéké for his news, and he came on the line to say that he was feeling better, but he talked as if he were out of breath. He said he was feeling very emotional after reading, in a book by his poet Mamadou Traoré Diop of Ouagadougou (picked up at the flea market where I found Gustave Désuet), a Mandingo mass for black African funerals.

I pray you, I beg you
Do me no honors
That I do not want
Above all do not weep over the dead
You must laugh, you must smile
Because to die is to live well
Among the ancestors who are so alive.

Thereupon Habéké invited me, after supper, to the old shed in his yard, to come and see the flute he had carved from the dedjené's long bone, and his mask of charred faces inspired by Mekkonen the Magnificent's skull. He also said that he would sing to offer wandering spirits a face in which to dwell, as in an Ityopya rediscovered, and he would play music for the sacred dance of the elder who had been rescued from oblivion.

Twelve

THAT NIGHT I rode my bicycle, with its flat tire, onto rue Lanthier where my dream slumbered in a shoe box, a white bungalow where all the windows were aglow as night was coming on. I laid my bike down on the asphalt driveway, and I rang the bell. Odile half opened the door and my heart leapt when I saw her. She was chewing a mouthful of dessert amid the din of the TV set and questioned me with her girl's wide-open eyes. Mumbling, I invited her to go with me to Habéké's, and she asked me to wait a minute. Voices echoed inside the house, Philippe and Marilou's heads, with their milk moustaches, appeared at the kitchen window. I greeted them, then another head came into view, a woman's head, frizzy and thicker, and finally Odile came out. She went to fetch her bicycle in the yard, and a moment later we were walking down the street.

"Was that your mother staring at us through the window?"

"It couldn't have been my father, I don't have one anymore..."

"You have no more father!"

"My father decided he wanted another woman, not my mother, and different children, so I decided to have no more father. He can go to hell, the bastard!"

That gave me a turn, what with my searching for my own father, while Odile, faced with the adult era's grave problems, had done hers in without a second thought. I would have liked to talk with her about this mystery, but she had Habéké on her mind, and wasn't interested in me.

"How is he doing? What was wrong with him?"

"He's not doing badly at the moment, but I don't know what got to him, he didn't tell me."

We lengthened our steps, and at the street corner we climbed onto our bicycles to pick up speed. We rolled side by side, she round and me squarish, and out of the corner of my eye I saw her face, a bright profile up against the world's darkness. Her hair was afloat, as long as sleepless nights, her ringed fingers gripped the handlebars, and my heart broke at the sight of all the beauty that was eluding me—and this was not the whim of a child on the run. It was the anguish of a man unhappy with his fate.

"Is it really true that you got married?"

She couldn't seem to get over it, and, discomfited, I said yes, as if it hurt. Odile confessed that she would have given a lot to attend the wedding, but I didn't reply. In Africa polygamy is widespread, and Odile would surely be able to attend another of Habéké's marriages, but I didn't want to turn the knife in her womanly wound.

Oh Odile, I said to myself, oh my Odile, first among women, from where have they come, all those rings glimmering like afflictions in my night? Were they the vows of other boys?

We leaned our bicycles against a tree in the Godins' yard. Through the shed's windows, strange lights were projecting fantastical shadows onto the walls. Odile and I pushed open the door. It moved, creaking on its hinges.

"Habéké, are you there?"

An oil lamp and candles shed a little light around the worktable, and all seemed calm in the shadows.

Suddenly a god plunged from the sky through the attic's trap door.

Odile cried out and we retreated into a corner of the shed to hide behind some garden chairs. I'd jumped out of my skin, but I recognized Habéké by the color of his legs. Later I learned that he had climbed into the attic to wait for me, like a child gestating in the belly of the universe, and that he wanted to be reborn before my eyes when I arrived.

"I'm scared," Odile whispered, "I want to go."

We were immobilized by Habéké, who was wriggling his hips, totally naked, his family jewels in the air, and his body smeared with magical colors. He'd donned the goalie's mask we'd brought back from Ityopia along with Mekkonen's bones, but he'd given himself a burnished face that reminded you of a sun or a lion's head, with bits of wool and hay glued ray-like around the sides. And Habéké had bracelets on his wrists, a feather necklace, a little tom-tom on his right hip. He was slapping its skin with his lithe hands in an African rhythm, as if the continent were exploding inside him, and suddenly I saw that he had chains on his ankles, small chains from a child's swing, evoking his people's enslaved past. Then Habéké started to sing complaints in Amharic, doleful as a famine sun, inviting the spirits to descend and dwell in his mask's house and to work their way into our world of flesh and bone. The mask's mouth was red thanks to the blood bedewing the living and infusing the words handed down generation after generation. A pipe hung from his lips, sculpted from a piece of wood resembling a baobab, and as his cries regaled the sky and all its dead, Habéké arched his back, undulating to the tom-tom's beat. His torso swept wide, his wild mane whipped through the air.

I later learned that in his moaning Habéké was chanting the caesarian birth of a universe via a goddess-mother who died in labor, and that all the cosmos' suns, too blazing to pass through the Woman's natural passage, had split the belly's skin to emerge like a necklace of fiery pearls, and this was the origin of all children's navels, a product of the world mother's mortal wound.

Now Habéké became wilder still and began to cry louder, as if he were being reborn along with his elder rescued from obscurity, and I heard him calling on the balanza and the tatagu kononi. He was dancing now in a frenzy, his body bathed in sweat where the fire was gleaming, and his hair flared out in volleys of raging serpents. Odile trembled at my shoulder, and I felt as if Habéké's songs and the beating of that little drum were bewitching me bit by bit.

Suddenly the tom-tom and the cries ceased: the spirits had consented to enter the shed and Odile and I were paralyzed with fear. Before us, the masked face turned toward the sky, and Habéké surrendered himself to the silent beings that had come out of the oppressive night.

"It's the spirits," I murmured.

I could swear that I could see them, so strong was my belief, I could have sworn it on the head and the blood of my true mother, but Odile saw nothing.

"What spirits? Where?"

"There! The lights flying around his head!"

Habéké had set down his pipe to begin blowing into his bone flute, strident notes that tore at one's ears, and it was then that I saw him with my own eyes.

"The ancestor! I see the ancestor!"

Odile tried to make out the spirit flickering at the tip of my finger, but she still saw nothing, and I cried again:

"It's him! Mekkonen the dedjené!"

Terrified, Odile freed herself from our hiding place to bolt toward the shed's door, but in her haste she tripped and as she fell she struck Habéké who knocked over the oil lamp, which shattered on the floor. A stream of fiery liquid collided with a pile of old newspapers. A few seconds later flames were licking at the walls as high up as the ceiling and were circling the can of gasoline and the lawnmower. The smoke attacked our eyes and throat, it was pure hell that we saw before us. Tangled up in rakes and the hammock, I had trouble getting out of my rat hole, but when I finally emerged my escape was blocked by a wall of fire. Odile was screaming at the top of her lungs, Habéké was rolling on the ground like a drunkard, and I felt my clothes burning on my skin. I grabbed a hoe and broke a window. Then I seized Odile by the shoulders to throw her through the window and I lifted Habéké, all I could see of him now was his dripping and rounded behind, and I pushed him too through the window frame, after which I had just enough time to launch myself into the opening. The rest was a whirl-wind of fire and cries and sirens in the night, and shadows dancing before my eyes. I tried to say something about the ancestor, but the mad silhouettes paid no heed. So I started to dream, I fell through the night and past the stars, I plunged into the sun where there dwelt a giant, the giant swallowed me up and I tumbled into his entrails, traversed his entire being and dropped into his man-shaped heart, and he killed me, he killed me, and I was dead.

When I woke, someone I didn't know was leaning over me, asking how many of us were in the shed. I saw again Odile,

Habéké, the elder Mekkonen, the ancestors and the dedjenés, and I murmured, with a whisper:

"We were thousands..."

Thirteen

ODILE AND I SPENT two days in the hospital thanks to our cuts, burns, and the smoke that had collected in our lungs. That's when I saw that my forearm had been sliced open by a piece of glass. Habéké had to stay there for two weeks as he was the one most affected given his nudity, particularly vulnerable when you're in hell. His burns were more serious than ours, but the mask he wore that night shielded his face—though perhaps too it was Mekkonen the dedjené who had saved him from the fire.

Of course, this juicy story had tongues wagging. We were even honored with our pictures in the newspaper, along with a photo of the shed, now a cindered ruin. A journalist of sorts talked to Mabiké Aksoune and Odile Francoeur and Hugues Paradis, although he ought to have reversed our names. Even though we described everything as we remembered it, the rumor spread of satanic rites and black magic, sorcery and the accursed plot of blacks, and when my semi-parents tried to persuade me to undergo a psychological examination, I could have killed them.

One morning, Odile and I were once more on the street

corner, Odile with her hair gone up in smoke, me with stitches in my arm. She was surrounded by friends, all commiserating with her as a girl burned alive, but I was being shunned like the plague and I found myself alone on my bench, while the handsome Alexandre was all over her. Oh, Odile talked to me, she hadn't completely abandoned me, but it was Habéké who she wanted to know about, Habéké who had given her the fright of her life in the shed, but who bewitched her with his unimaginable Africa.

Every night, after school, I boycotted the bus that was there to bring us home, and walked the distance in the autumn weather, which allowed me to mourn Odile's coolness, but above all to visit Habéké in the hospital.

At first my friend had to stay in bed, and he resembled a mummified pharaoh with his torso and arms all swathed in cloth. Madame Godin was often there, in an armchair at Habéké's bedside. She spent her time going over and over what had happened, a Kleenex tucked into her bodice, rolled into a ball: and sometimes Monsieur Godin leafed nervously through a newspaper. When I poked my nose into the room, the Godins rose and left us alone, Habéké and me, so we might fraternize in peace.

The first time I saw my friend after his ritual dance of love in honor of his elder, I was afraid. I wondered whether he was himself again, if he had not left parts of his soul in the land of the dead, but he seemed indeed to be the friend I knew, with all his wits about him. He explained that it was normal in an African trance to oneself become the mask amidst the spirits, himself a spirit among the dedjené, and it was even the precondition for a successful ceremony. He claimed to have remembered everything except the fire, so I told him the whole story, only I didn't mention that I'd saved his skin.

"How did we end up on the lawn, the three of us?"

I was silent on the subject because I despised vanity, and above all I didn't want Habéké to owe me his life, given the burden of such a debt. That is how we found ourselves once more blood brothers, alive and on the road to scarring and healing.

"I saw it, it's ugly, real crocodile skin."

"It's better than no skin at all, my brother."

I was the only one who made Habéké laugh, and that made him feel good even if it hurt because of the new skin that did not like being stretched into a smile, but one night, not laughing, I confessed that outside the room everyone was giving us dirty looks as if they wanted to kill us, whether in the streets, the school, or even the hospital. They claimed we were possessed by the devil, and I told him I wanted to escape, to vanish without leaving an address, but Habéké urged me to calm down, and above all not to leave without him. That appeased me a little, but back home I began to seethe, and to dream of exile. That is how one night, on TV, I came across a program where they were talking about a man who at first reminded me of Gustave Désuet, a Russian novelist called Aleksandr Solzhenitsyn. I learned that his father died before he was born in 1918, that he was decorated during the war after studying physics and philosophy, that later he was to renounce his nationality, but in the meantime Aleksandr endured a four-year exile for having dared to put down on paper all he decried when it came to one man, Russia's Little Father, and then there was a second exile in a concentration camp where he spent eight years mulling over the suffering that would later surface in the novels he culled from his memories. In the end he was thrown out of Russia for good, stripped of his passport, and the poor man turned up in Switzerland with his Nobel Prize all crumpled, poised for a new life. No one knew what would happen to him, since that was the end of the documentary. Life had to start up again, and history to be made.

The fact remains that that night I had the vision of an exceptional man who was intimate with the secrets of exile.

The next day I told Habéké about Alexandr Solzhenitsyn's eventful life, and he could hardly believe his ears. When I shared with him my plan to write to this man and ask him about the possibilities of a life in exile, a wave of hope surged through Habéké's being, which he felt even on the surface of his skin.

"Yes, you must write him immediately, do you know where he lives?"

"In Switzerland or in exile, it's the same thing."

"Find something to write with, and we'll write him!"

That night I wrote on hospital paper, with a hospital pen, a letter to the man we had baptized with the beautiful name of spiritual father. We told him that we had almost died seeking a better world, but we would die in any case if we did not find it. We talked to him about the tree of life on the island of our dreams, of Habéké's lost Africa and Mekkonen the dedjené, exile in the world of the spirits, of my eyes that come from China and everything else, and we wanted him to bless us with a future.

> *... you who had the courage to live in your hard cold*
>   *Russia, you, all of whose*
> *books we will try to read, we are asking you for some*
>   *of your strength to help us*
> *not to die young in the Accident we abhor and we*
>   *want you to show us where we*
> *may find exile and its island that saves men like you,*
>   *and how to live there and*
> *create a people without the hypocrisy of the adult*
>   *era...*

The next day I rushed to get to the post office before it closed. Breathless, I bought a special envelope that can cross an ocean, I had our words weighed casually by a postman, and then I licked the stamps, which tasted terrible, but that is how a sliver of our hope was able to take to the skies.

Alexandre Solzhenitsyn
Russian writer
Exile (Switzerland)
AIR MAIL

Fourteen

THE FOLLOWING WEEK, as Habéké was feeling better, they said he could get up if his heart was in it, and his heart was so much in it that he began to circulate among the sick, but Habéké could not imagine that this life would lead him so far, into a new universe you can't see from the street, another world on high of eternal suffering like a heaven on earth, but it's a hospital heaven populated by the feverish and the dying, where my friend was introduced to the destinies that now haunted him all day long.

That is how one afternoon I found Habéké in the visitors' room with a girl who from a distance I took to be Odile, but when I rushed over I found myself saying hello to a stranger in a wheelchair, a young girl our age who seemed very nice with her short straight hair, her gentle smile, and her fluffy slippers. She didn't seem very sick, but when she opened her mouth to respond to my greeting, I saw that she had no life force at all.

"This is Nathalie," Habéké said.

She was desperately trying to tell me something, but her words slipped away somewhere between her heart and her mouth, powerless to reach her lips. Later, Habéké told me about Nathalie's misfortune. She suffered from a terrible drought, as in distant deadly Africa, because of clots in her brain, accretions of detritus that blocked her blood vessels, and the illness was inching her toward death, as if an evil Harmattan wind, trapped inside her, was churning constantly inside her body, and destroying it.

"They say it's all over, there's no more hope..."

I couldn't believe that this sweet girl smiling at me was awaiting her final day, with her parents sleeping there, in the hospital, amid medicinal odours, their dreams filled with who knows what horrors. It was a tragedy, a terrible destiny that I rejected with all my soul and all my human strength.

"But we won't let her die..."

Habéké couldn't be more right: the doctors had given up and the parents would do the same tomorrow, but we, we would not abandon Nathalie to those pathetic people who had lost hope and were killing her prematurely, seeing that no one can survive in a world without beliefs, but Habéké and I believed in miracles, and we would free Nathalie from death to restore life to her in all its glory, there where she had her place with us in the flow of generations. We would succeed, we were sure, given that we possessed the necessary powers. I saw the infinite aglow in the eyes of Habéké, my only brother who, when he saw Nathalie, talked to her about his much-loved Africa, and all his cherished departed, but above all about how he survived despite God's drought and the cruelty of men, because he wanted to urge her to believe and to be reborn into a new world and into the beauty of exile and its dreams.

"Elsewhere," Habéké murmured to her. "Far off... beyond the horizon, we must always look away, imagine things differently, and you are there... over there... with us..."

Then Habéké shared with me his heart's secret, now mine as well.

"I promised her we would save her."

AS DAYS WENT BY, the prospect of saving Nathalie shone brightly in our minds, and together we wracked our brains to find a way. In the first place, how could we distract her parents, who were living there night and day? And then how to sneak Nathalie out of a hospital with grills on its windows, and where surveillance was constant? And even if we got her out, what to do with her afterwards, lost as we would be on the street? Where to take her? Where to hide her? How to take care of this poor girl? The obstacles seemed insurmountable, but we persevered so stubbornly that even in school my mind constantly wandered in search of a brilliant inspiration.

Often, in my discouragement, I was dying to open myself to Odile, to welcome her into the realm of our deepest secrets where she would be enthroned alongside Nathalie, but I hid away all my strivings and my mysteries. It was still too early to reveal my dream life, but the hour would come, I had to be wise enough to be patient.

Finally, despite how hard it is for humans to be intelligent, it was Habéké who came up with a plan so amazing that even the very best bandits wouldn't have thought of it.

"It's fantastic," he whispered to me one night in the visitors' room, "things are falling into place all by themselves, like magic, and it's beautiful, starting with Nathalie who really wants us to save her, her eyes cry it out to me every day, she wants us to take her where we will and to do what we think is best for her. You and I are going to spirit her away..."

I was dazzled as if by a sun, by the sun of a friend's life to be saved, and I wanted to lead Nathalie into exile with Odile and Habéké, but I had to start by calming myself, I knew that Habéké was being released from the hospital the next day, Saturday, and that Nathalie's parents had received permission to bring their daughter home a week later, since the medical treatments were ending, and we had to plan what next to do. Nathalie would be going home the following Friday to reunite with her possessions, her bed and her dreams, waiting to see— but to see what? To see death's shadows rolling over her, that was accepted and understood, but what was so wonderful was that we, Habéké and I, would appear bringing light, and we would change the world.

"You know where we could take her?"

"Where?"

"To the chalet..."

The more I thought about it, the more brilliant the idea seemed, the chalet, by the calm dreamlike river, under a welcoming sky.

"My parents boarded it up for the winter, but all we have to do is to take the panel off the door, and there's everything you could want inside, bedding, preserves, wood for the stove."

"We'll bring books, paper to write a diary or poems, perhaps a letter to Solzhenitsyn..."

"What's most important," Habéké said, "is to give her gris-gris to repel the sickness's evil spirits."

We will leave Mekkonen the Dedjené's bones with her so that the elder will watch over her, and Habéké will make her a mask to channel the becalmed spirits coming to earth, the only ones who can correct the opaque imbalances at the root of our troubles: then within the chalet, and even in the surrounding countryside, we will track down the dangerous talismans, and only then will Nathalie be able to cleanse herself through solitude and reflection, bathed in the light of the ancestors' vital forces, so she will heal completely, and for good. Afterwards we will take her with us to the island of exile and yoke our suns to its earth and to the earth of Odile. But Habéké, while we waited, with his soul of a soothsaying healer and medicine man, wanted us to submerge ourselves in pharmacopoeia to prepare a miraculous cure for Nathalie that would dissolve her clots and have her blood flowing as before, that would give her back her speech and her life. When she will be cured, Habéké said, then we will baptise her with a new name to free her from the shadow of evil, and will declare to the scourge's spirits that she has conquered the ailing body to which they had condemned her, and that she now reigns over a new body, pure and sacrosanct, like a fetish.

"We will call her Schla Maryam..."

The Image of Mary. That would suit her well, like a light in the eyes and joy on a face.

We dreamed of the day when Nathalie would once more be a power.

*

THE NEXT DAY, Habéké left the hospital with onion peel on his shoulders.

"Did you see?" he said to me, baring his chest. "Beautiful budding baby skin I picked up at the nursery!"

"But the baby's black, they picked the right color to restore you."

We laughed, happy to find ourselves in the open air, but we had things to do: a life to save and a world to change.

That night I ate at Habéké's to celebrate his return, and Monsieur and Madame Godin seemed at last to have come to terms with what had happened. As soon as we got up from the table we rode our bikes to the local library to explore the plant encyclopedias and immerse ourselves in pharmacopeia. We combed through them until closing time and went back the next day. We were able to find decoctions that we could put our hands on, rhubarb leaves and wild chicory, autumn leaves that abounded along the rail line.

In the afternoon we cut down wild burdock under a fine rain, looking like two druids lost in the undergrowth. The next day was fine, and we harvested chicory sprays that open their big blue eyes only in the sun, batting their lashes. And it was at my house, in the old garage, that we tied them up with string and hung them upside down from the ceiling to dry.

On Monday, in the bus and at school, Habéké was greeted like the oddity he'd always been, except by Odile, who could not get over the worshipful ceremony he'd dedicated to Mekkonen the dedjené. Alexandre, meanwhile, looked on, gimlet-eyed, his nose out of joint from jealousy. It was strange to see Habéké sitting peacefully, leaning back in his seat, not stark naked, not smeared with colors, not possessed by fiery spirits and voracious ancestors. He was there, placid, as in class where he worked studiously, and if he had not been black he wouldn't even have been noticeable up against the school's white walls, but in his head as in mine there was a furor of secret lives where all was sun-lit with ideals.

Every afternoon that week, despite the coming night, we went to gather the last bog rhubarb and the last blue bouquets. Thursday night we went to visit Nathalie in the hospital to see if life was following its course. Our friend was stretched out in bed, still clinging to this life we were going to save for her, with visitors surrounding her. They saw us through the half- opened door, but we vanished as if spirited away.

The next night Nathalie left the hospital, and Habéké and I couldn't sit still. After dinner we took off on our bicycles and walked them into the shadows where our friend's house stood, near the bus station. It was a bungalow, a little like Odile's, but more expensive, in stone, with trees, and two cars parked in the lane. All the windows were shining bright into the night and shadows were moving to and fro inside. You sensed that there was life there, but the true life at the core of this life was Nathalie. Habéké and I looked at each other. In our eyes you could see that we would stop at nothing.

That night we stuffed our bags with rhubarb leaves and dried chicory, and, feverish with excitement, looked forward to the following day.

Later, in bed, I opened Gustave Désuet's *Lives Dreamed*, and fell asleep to "Open Eyes."

> *"Are you looking at me*
> *Or your reflection atremble in my eyes?"*
> *"But I am neither me nor my trembling reflection*
> *Because I am you and I am your eyes*
> *I am your arid heart that would never want to be*
>   *loved*
> *I am your eyes that will not have seen me*
> *Your eyes that are seas to the madman and his thirst"*

*

I OPENED MY EYES onto a night that was like a prenatal luminescence. I opened my eyes, and I thought it was a miracle. In the midst of this miracle I rose onto the tips of my toes and dressed warmly. Crossing the kitchen, I grabbed a banana that I ate on the way to Habéké's house, where he was waiting in the darkness. We were too anxious to speak, we just left. Twenty minutes later we were at Nathalie's.

All was dark and calm in the streets. Nathalie's house, like the others, seemed lost in a deep sleep, and the city was a dream wherein we drifted. When we slipped between the cedar hedge and the car, we saw a silhouette through the side door window. I recognized Nathalie, who was waiting with her coat and little boots, a wool bonnet on her head. Quietly, we brought her out of the house and led her gently through the streets. I felt her weakness as she leaned against us, almost weightless, and we had to support her or she would have collapsed.

Fortunately, the terminal was not far. By seven o'clock we were in a bus, thanks to our pocket money, along with a dozen sleeping passengers, me sitting with Nathalie who had pulled up her coat collar to hide her face, Habéké farther on, alone, feigning not to know us in order to cover our tracks and confuse witnesses.

Nathalie moved not a muscle, but I felt her aura, its physical presence. I saw her out of the corner of my eye, she was watching the countryside file by the dirty window, and I wondered what she might be thinking, leaving behind everything she knew and those she loved. I wondered if perhaps she didn't want to follow us, but with a lump in my throat, I didn't know how to talk to her.

Three quarters of an hour later the bus dropped us off at a crossroads, beside a roadside cross where a messiah was eternally dying. The chalet was five minutes away on the left. To the right, I saw the railroad bridge beams from which we'd launched ourselves toward the sun one summer's day. We walked through the wayside stones and I recognized the place even though there were almost no leaves left on the trees, which changed its aspect. An icy drizzle was falling, crackling onto our clothes, and the chalet by the water seemed sad, abandoned for the winter. When we took the familiar pebbled path, I felt my heart twinge at the sight of Habéké's chalet, all boarded up, beneath the great naked trees with their twisted branches. There was no longer any sense of Damas in the prune tree, nor of Babylon in the willows, nor of Persia in the lilacs, but everywhere there was still the immense purifying solitude in which the emptied world was bathed.

We sat Nathalie down on the edge of the well, and while I rubbed her arms to warm them, Habéké took a hammer from his bag to pry off the panel over the back door, which we pushed to enter the chalet.

"I'll take off a window panel too."

No sooner said than done, and a window was opened onto the gray river, covered as far as the eye could see with little bubbles, thanks to the pecking rain.

As soon as her shoes and coat were off, Nathalie lay down on the old sofa smelling of mice, and fell asleep. Habéké and I made a fire in the stove, then went out to hunt down dangerous talismans. We spent two hours searching around the chalet, in the bushes and hedges, in the ditches and the brush on the riverbanks where we had married. We even climbed into the trees and onto the chalet roof. We gathered up shards from bottles and a child's mitt; rusted nails and a coat button; a spoke from a bicycle wheel and the tag from a roaming dog; a snake's shed skin and the bodies of a perch and a blackbird; and even an unhatched egg in a bird's nest. As soon as we re-entered the chalet we tossed all those evil talismans into the fire, and right after found a dead fieldmouse in the shed and rat poison under the kitchen sink. We threw those little prophets of doom into the flames.

"We can't even talk about devil's rhubarb," said Habéké, "because some words are also dangerous talismans. We're going to call it now by its other name, croquia."

Just then Nathalie opened her eyes, and I felt strange: by this time her parents would have found her empty bed, the pain we were inflicting on those poor people made me feel bad, but then I thought of their joy at soon finding their child cured, and tears came to my eyes. While I was still overcome by these thoughts, Habéké had taken water from the pump and had put it to boil to prepare the first magical infusions of croquia and chicory.

While the water was heating, we pushed a big armchair up to the stove and we installed Nathalie in it like a queen, beneath a mound of blankets. I helped her to settle into the cushions so she could admire the river running past the window, beneath the reflection of her face at rest. You see, I told her in secret, you see, oh Nathalie of all my hopes, the river of blood must flow through you, softly, like a passing dream, to imbue you with its life... the life where you are no longer alone... for you have friends... and we are here...

Meanwhile Habéké had unzipped his bag and I saw him place on a table Mekkonen the dedjené's piece of skull and a handful of gris-gris—a feather, an oyster shell, his carnelian necklace, his rain bracelet, his knuckle bones, a little gold cross with a handle, which symbolized life.

"This week," said Habéké, "you will eat nothing, but you will drink an enormous amount, only infusions, to wash away the sickness. The magical chicory will purify your blood and cleanse it, and the miraculous croquia will dissolve your clots."

Habéké then pulled from his bag a string mask that he had himself sculpted in Styrofoam and painted with water colours, the head of a red bird with a black beak and a blue and yellow crest, a tatagu kononi, the totem of fertility that would protect Nathalie and would lure to the chalet genies of the air and rain, but also the spirit of the sun, which endows every human being with light and shadow that can be of service, or do harm, and it is in meditation and prayer that Nathalie will learn to leave darkness behind her and embrace the light.

"Never forget the contributions of the earth and the spirits," said Habéké, "because the life that is in you was taken from somewhere when you were born, high up in the cosmos where there was an opening created in the air between the stars, and all those holes made in the universe by our lives must be filled with our gifts, or the universe, all gnawed away, will collapse in a roar of stars and that will be the end of the world..."

A smile appeared at the corner of Nathalie's mouth, she understood Habéké's teachings. I thought that we had done well to bring her to this lost place, and I could sense, deep down, my belief in life and in a supernatural power.

The kettle began to whistle on the stove, and I prepared the infusions we would share with Nathalie, whose face was pale with fatigue, but who smiled as she watched us. Her waxen hand hung beyond the covers, and I saw in this hand a world's fruiting, the precious fruit of immortality that we disregard and destroy, and I don't know what came over me, but I touched Nathalie's feverish hand, I caressed it and I softly stroked it with kisses, then I tucked it into the warmth of the blankets, and I again kissed Nathalie on her cheek and in her hair. Then I poured boiling water into the cups where the medicinal herbs swirled.

While gazing at the clouds sending down rain onto the river, we drank our preparation of tea, then Habéké, who thought what I was thinking, turned to Nathalie to ask her if she wanted us to take her back home. She said no, shaking her head.

That is when Habéké and I looked at each other sadly, since the hour had come for us to leave Nathalie alone in the chalet. We got up without knowing what to say, because we wanted to stay, but too long an absence would have betrayed us. We promised Nathalie to return and spend the next day with her, and she again smiled, she smiled at us all the time. She had no fear, she knew that the good spirits would watch over her, and so we kissed her hands, her cheeks, her brow, her neck, the corner of her mouth. We lingered for so long that we had to race to catch the bus in the village.

My last image from this day was Nathalie with her hair ruffled and her eyes burning, sunk into the armchair near the stove, buried under blankets with the gris-gris, Mekkonen the dedjené's skull fragment, and the tatagu kononi mask facing her, while she contemplated the river without moving. Then the road gleaming in the rain as we ran, casting long looks, one after the other, behind us, I see again the boarded-up chalet exhaling through its chimney a pathetic wisp of smoke, the little chalet alone in the grayness, smothered under the clouds of rain, falling back beyond the tree branches and the hedges, then disappearing from sight as we vanished at the first curve in the road.

Fifteen

THAT NIGHT, in our traumatized town, word spread that a sick adolescent had disappeared from her home and was being sought everywhere. Given her condition it was an abduction that was feared, rather than a flight; the parents had to suspect a friend of the family or a suspicious-looking neighbor who however had done nothing, perhaps even an unbalanced nurse who had spotted her prey at the hospital, but an abduction without a break-in or violence, was that still an abduction?

Habéké and I were very sorry to be hurting these desperate people, raising painful questions in their minds, but they were the ones who lacked faith, not us, and it had to be their hearts that were afflicted with this despair, not ours, because our hearts had faith. But the pain would not last long, and soon light would sweep away the shadows, though we could not yet reveal the truth to one and all, it was too soon, the world would not understand. We had to let the miracle do its work, to let it operate, abetted by kindly minds.

Yes, it was still too early, but at the same time, not quite, not for everyone: there was one person who had to be told about our revelation, yes, one only, and that is how Habéké and I found ourselves once again on rue Lanthier.

"That's it," I said to myself, walking beside Habéké. "That's it, it's happened, it's happened to us..."

We stopped in front of Odile's house, long enough to take deep breaths and to consider the importance of what we were doing, then we plunged further into the night to go and ring at the side door. The naked bulb went on over our heads, and Odile appeared with her short hair, singed by the fire where we had all been burned together. Her eyes asked fearfully what we were doing there, wandering about like animals.

"You have to come with us," I said.

"Where? To do what?"

"We have secrets to share with you," said Habéké. "You have to follow us."

Uneasy, seeing us so teeming with mysteries, Odile hesitated in the doorway. Her large dark eyes stared at us and questioned us, but in the end she gave in and followed. We walked to the end of rue Lanthier where it met a park, all in shadow, and there our friend sat down on a swing, facing us, while we remained standing.

"What is it? What do you want?"

Habéké opened his mouth first.

"Have you heard about a sick girl who has been kidnapped?"

Odile's face changed color.

"Well, it's us."

"What, us?"

"We're the ones who took her away."

Hearing these words, Odile burst out laughing, so I spoke in my turn.

"It's true that it's us, and her name is Nathalie, that girl is our friend, and Habéké knew her in the hospital, but it's not what you think, we didn't take her by force, we just helped her to walk to where she wanted to go, and tonight she's doing well, she's healing in a hiding place no one knows about..."

"I don't believe you."

"Don't believe us if you don't want to," said Habéké, "but it's the truth, and don't cry over it, no, you have to thank heaven because it's good news, it's something marvelous, we're talking about a rebirth..."

That was the last straw for Odile, who lasered us with her eyes, shouting that we must be sick to be inventing such stories, that we had no right to be taking advantage of other people's misfortunes just in order to be noticed, and I think that at that point she had us shaking in our boots, Odile, and we proposed that she go with us the next morning, at seven o'clock at the terminal, so we could bring her into the light where she would see the truth through her own eyes, where she would understand the good we were doing in the shadows, aided by the elder's life force, and all the great geniuses of the atmosphere and the dedjené's of Ityopya. That having been said, the fierce Odile rose from the swing in a clattering of chains and took long strides homeward. Following on her heels, we swore that we needed her in order to live, that she and Nathalie could go forth to remake the world in the island of·exile, leaving behind our paltry lives as they presented themselves in the poisonous Accident, our lives imperiled by the hate, the despair, and the hypocrisy of the adult era, to go and found together, the four of us, a new people, imbued with peace and hope, on the other side of things, because in finding Nathalie we had at last reached an equilibrium, found the missing pillar for our sky, the star missing from our constellation. It's then that Habéké seized Odile by the arm and forced her to stop. On the asphalt, with a rock, he traced a sign I'd never seen, a sort of r surmounted by an umlaut, and he said that it was the figure three amongst the scorched faces, an evil figure, a frail figure that wanted to reach the sky and immortality without first having conquered and purified the earth, and it was the emblem of mankind's end and the end of the world, the dangerous talisman hidden in great numbers by the spirit of pestilence, and before Nathalie we were three and still cursed, but now we were four and from now on we would be saved and at last able to give the gift of life, to go forth and create the universe with our dreams. And so Habéké traced in the asphalt the figure four of Ityopya's scorched faces, and that unsettled me, not just Odile, I too felt my legs tremble when I saw the figure four of scorched faces, the perfect figure veiled in the infinite by totems and by spirits; four, which, as fate would have it, is the other number for God.

Among the burned faces of Ityopya, four is written: ô.

Sixteen

ON SUNDAY MORNING, at dawn, Habéké and I thought we were entering a dream when we entered the bus station: Odile was waiting for us, sitting stiffly on a bench, her face clearly showing that she'd had no sleep. Seeing us, she lowered her eyes. Habéké, who had stolen money from his parents, bought three tickets at the wicket, after which we approached Odile, who told us right off, snatching her ticket from Habéké's hands, that she didn't want to talk to us.

We left her there and went to sit at the other end of the terminal.

When we got into the bus, Odile slid onto the seat beside the driver, while Habéké and I headed for the back, where my friend soon fell asleep to the purring of the motor. I stayed awake, observing from afar Odile's somber mien, her head aswarm with uncertainties. She still didn't believe us and was accompanying us just to see with her own eyes how far we could go in lying and cruelty, but I feared nothing and I was anxious to see her fall on her knees when she encountered the truth and gentleness of our world.

Then I dozed off amid the fumes of gasoline, and I opened my eyes just before the village, to rouse Habéké.

"Wake up! We're here!"

Hearing us coming along the aisle, Odile rose in her turn. We got out at the same crossroads as the day before, at the foot of the same cross where the same poor bloodied Christ was still wracked with pain.

All three of us stood there amid the stones, watching the bus pull away, then Habéké and I started off. Odile let us go ahead before following. We felt her at our back like a shadow, like a threat or a guilty conscience, we heard her stepping through the pebbles, when all of a sudden, at a turn, the chalet appeared through the bare branches. We began to walk faster with our hearts pounding in our chests, and seeing that there was no more smoke coming from the chimney, we started to run. In my stampede I saw the landscape breaking up, the chalet pulsating before my eyes, jolted by a trembling world, and in my fear I anticipated the worst, but when we charged through the back door we found Nathalie there, who seemed not to have moved an inch since the night before. Her eyes open, she was reclined in her armchair, under the blankets swathing her in wool. We approached gently and she raised her head to show us her smile, then we got down on our knees to ask her how she was doing and to murmur sweet things, to touch her face and hands. All warm and quivering, she smiled and her eyes betrayed her joy at seeing us again.

Soon after, when I went to get fresh water from the pump, I found Odile standing in the doorway. I don't know what was at work in her face, perhaps rage or disgust, in any case she could not bear what she saw and took off.

"Let her go," said Habéké, "let her run, she'll get tired and then she'll come back."

He was right: a half hour later, as we were feeding Nathalie a magical infusion, Odile returned to the chalet, furious, her face white and her eyes blazing.

"This can't be! It makes no sense! You can't do this!! You understand?"

She knocked over a lamp and threw herself in our direction.

"You're crazy! You're going to kill her!"

She was slow to come to her senses, but we tried to reason with her, to talk to her calmly and to once more explain everything, but she didn't want to hear and she fled again. Dear Nathalie did not take well to these wild cries and agitation.

"Okay," I said to Habéké, "I'm going to talk to her."

I went out to find Odile, who was sitting in the grass a bit farther on, leaning against the wooden shed, trembling with rage.

"Don't come near me, you bloody madman!"

I went up to her anyway, telling her she was wrong, that she didn't know how to see the truth.

"The truth," she said, "is that you're going to kill her!"

"If we bring her back home, what do you think they're going to do?"

"I don't know... they're going to care for her, comfort her, they'll..."

Odile began to sob.

"No," I said, "they're not going to care for her, they're going to let her die because they have no more hope, they're just waiting for her to die because for them it's over, while we're going to save her, we have miraculous potions, we have all the magic of the ancestors and the dedjené, and we have cleared the surroundings of all the dangerous talismans, the good spirits of rain and fertility are going to chase away the bad spirits of sickness and the scourges..."

I talked like that for a long time to teach Odile how to see the reality hidden behind her own universe, to see the higher world that enfolds our own in its crown of glory. I don't know what she was thinking, she didn't say a word, but in the end she seemed somewhat calmer when I asked her to give us a week to prove ourselves. If Nathalie was not miraculously cured by the end of that week, I promised we would return her to her parents.

Nevertheless Odile was still crying, so I decided to go back to Nathalie and Habéké, hoping she would eventually join us, but she had a hard head, Odile. She spent all afternoon outside, ranting around the chalet. I decided that she needed more time to assimilate this amazing world she was just discovering thanks to us. For now, we had to busy ourselves with Nathalie, and we spent the day talking to her softly, caressing her, encouraging her. From time to time one of us fed the fire and prepared the miraculous infusions, warming a pot of water on the stove where croquia and chicory leaves were macerating. With this soothing essence we delicately washed her face, her shoulders, her arms, her throat, her legs, her feet, and then we massaged her hands and scalp, and Nathalie swooned under our caresses.

At one point dark clouds passed over, rain came down onto the chalet, and we thought then that Odile would come to us, but she stayed outside, shivering under the downpour.

The hours flew by, and soon we had to think about leaving. We piled up wood next to the stove, placed food on the table in case Nathalie got hungry, not forgetting water and the curative leaves, the gris-gris, the mask, and Mekkonen's skull fragment, then we tucked in our friend for the night.

"We're coming back, don't be afraid, we're always thinking of you."

I would come Tuesday, Habéké Thursday, and we would deal with school penalties and parental punishments.

"Two nights is nothing," I told Nathalie, "when you're asleep you don't see them, I mean what's left is just one day, tomorrow, and a day is nothing, it's like opening your eyes and closing them, and it's as if I were already back, that I'd never left..."

Nathalie smiled at the angels and we delayed our departure to embrace her once more. When we really had to leave, when we closed the door on her face, my heart was full to the brim with warmth and joy. Happy to be alive and to be walking in the countryside beside Habéké, I was dying for it to be Tuesday morning, with me next to Nathalie.

Odile shot out of the bushes and followed us at a distance along the road. When the bus arrived, she got on and sat behind the driver next to a woman, while Habéké and I went to the back where we had to separate, there being just four or five free places. I found myself beside a man reading a book about astronomy. One thing led to another, and he explained to me Baron Eötvös of Budapest's experiment, proving the rotation of the earth, and he talked to me about the comet Kohoutec that we would soon see passing across the sky.

At the terminal we got down after Odile because of passengers blocking the aisle. We had to run after her in the street.

"It's only a week," I told her when I caught up. "It's a promise, only a week..."

"You'll see," said Habéké, "in a little while Nathalie will receive her new life, and she'll be called Schla Maryam."

Odile walked all stiff like a rich woman, as if her ears were pierced.

"Schla Maryam!" Habéké cried after letting her go by. "Don't forget that name, Schla Maryam!"

Seventeen

M ONDAY MORNING, Odile was at our bus stop, but she had
death on her face and poison in her eyes. We tried to get
close to her to find out what was wrong, but she threw herself
into the arms of Alexandre, who told us to leave her alone, that
he didn't know what we had done to her, but that if we kept on
bothering her, he and his friends would wipe the floor with us.

Just then the bus arrived. Habéké and I sat down behind
the driver, and Odile went to the back with Alexandre.

"What's wrong with her?" I asked Habéké. "Do you think
that..."

"No, she won't say anything, I know it. It's just that it's
hard for her to learn new truths, but she won't talk, trust me,
she's on our side but she doesn't know it yet."

When we reached the school, Odile vanished into the
crowd, then Habéké again told me to trust him, and led me
to our locker, where we hung up our windbreakers and collected our books. I then saw that my hands were trembling.
Obsessed with Nathalie, I realized that I should not have been
at school that morning, the school that stifled me and was killing me, light years from my secret world, but that I ought to

have been back there, far away, living my authentic dream life in the boarded-up chalet, on the edge of life's river, embracing the perfumed hair and caressing the soft hand of a loved one.

*

It was past ten o'clock, and we were doing our math exercises. Sitting at his desk, Habéké was calculating away inside his head, while I was no longer in my books. I had left the world of equations to take to the skies where I was adrift in clouds, from where I saw, far down on the autumnal earth, the little gray chalet smoking among the trees, near the dark and meandering ribbon of water, and I said to myself: Oh Nathalie of my solitude and sadness, what are you doing at this moment as I think of you?

*

The classroom door suddenly burst open, to the astonishment even of our mathematics teacher. We recognized Monsieur Mafouz, the principal, an enormous, imposing Egyptian who scanned the students with his murderous gaze. When his eyes met those of Habéké, he commanded him to follow. Habéké didn't even pause to gather up his things, and he rose without looking at me. When I saw him disappear, I knew that he had entered a universe from which he would never return.

All the rest is a dream of death where the world breaks down.

Odile was in Monsieur Mafouz's office, in tears. Seeing her, Habéké admitted to everything, on the spot. He said that Odile had not lied and that Nathalie was indeed at the chalet, and Monsieur Mafouz leapt to his telephone. Soon after, two policemen turned up at the school with Monsieur and Madame Godin, sobbing; others, along with Nathalie's parents, found the young invalid at the chalet. In the newspaper that week there were huge, sensational headlines. Our entire town, overwhelmed, talked of nothing else but this senseless affair, of this poor cancerous child kidnapped by an unbalanced adolescent who stole money from his adoptive parents, and everyone recalled his obsession with witchcraft, black magic, and satanism.

As for me, frozen in my cataclysmic life, I expected to be arrested, hanged or shot, but no one came to handcuff me. Habéké swore that he had acted alone. And Odile didn't want to say anything more, perhaps because I had once saved her from the flames.

A week later Habéké was assigned for a year to a reformatory, a "center of readaptation for young people in trouble," and it's there that Habéké, troubled, would be readapted, he who had already been adapted earlier on, and I wondered if he would survive this barrage of supplementary reforms.

And I, emptied of life, my dreams in tatters like those of my ill-starred friends, I knew that I would now roam through the things of this world like a shadow of myself.

In October of that year I became one with the night.

Eighteen

A S I DON'T KNOW where to start, I'll begin at the beginning, and the beginning starts with the end of the world.

Yes, the apocalypse had begun, and it quietly made its way past the blinkered eyes of passers-by, just as Gustave Désuet had predicted, and I was the night, but I was not alone in the shadows as Odile and Habéké were careering down along with me. I have forgotten the first hours of the end of the world, up to that autumn morning when a weak sun showed itself through my curtains. I saw something stirring before me. My hands were writing. It was a letter, a letter to Habéké, in which I told him that everything was gone, that the sky had fallen in, as if he didn't know it.

That is how I came back to a kind of life, a life without outcries or purity, a barely normal existence, sedated like the end of time, where nothing moved, where nothing brightened the days or eclipsed the sun shared by the common man who wants no more than what makes it possible for him live at dandelion height.

One fine day of this new life, I burned a book.

Dear Habéké,

    *That's it: I've thrown Gustave Désuet into the
fire because I've started to know his poems too well.
I thought of you, of both of us, through the flames,
and it made me ill, but that's life, as we say when we
are defeated...*

I saw that it burned badly, the past, and the memories along
with it, given that there is always a residue, even afterwards,
there always remains something like a private pain, something
unseen that will never burn.

> *One would want you among all the loving women,*
> *In the place where you beg for the eucharist of beggars.*
> *Do you love only the dark water and the bread's chaff*
> *While scorning the stars that have fallen by the side*
>   *of your bed?*

> *It's that we love badly: to seek love is madness.*
> *Allow me to wish rather that I be well hated,*
> *Or was I without truly knowing it*
> *Among all those dead men one man alive.*

Farewell to you, quaint Gustave, cursed bastard poet. You
schooled me like only a true man could do, and to thank you I
burned you, but in the end you are eternal, and you know it well,
you son of a bitch. Your poems are engraved inside my eyelids.

> *We must kill*
> *All those I was without believing in them*
> *Only the one you loved*
> *The one worthy of belief*
> *Will survive me.*

Those were Gustave Désuet's last words, the poem that ends his *Lives Dreamed* that was going moldy in the flea market; after which, sad Gustave went to take his life at the end of a rope.

Dear Habéké,
I'm still trying to live and I'm behaving as if you were there, beside me, and I'm saying anything at all, playing the fool, like before, but I feel so alone...

And then it was Halloween. There was a costume ball at school, Friday night, and I disguised myself in the school bathroom, just before the party, that is I stripped all the way down except for my underpants, and when I entered the ballroom, the bedecked cafeteria, everyone froze. Almost naked, my skin blackened from toes to ears with shoe polish, I had a pickax on my shoulder and a pipe in my mouth, since I was Mekkonen the dedjené. Too bad, Odile didn't come to the party and that bothered me because I'd done it to impress her, but I forget if it was out of love or hate. At a certain point I left the cafeteria to roam the school's empty halls, barefoot in my underpants, bare-chested, black as a Black, with my ax and my pipe. I sang at the top of my voice my laments in an invented Amharic, and when I came face to face with the janitor on the second floor he was so scared that he let me go by and I was able to keep on drifting in the half-light, and raving, all through the school.

The next night was the real Halloween, the Halloween of the streets, with monsters everywhere in town and candies at the doors of all the houses. I went out with Jérome and Benoît who knew I was sad and wanted to cheer me up. Jérome was disguised as Thor, with his hammer of thunder and lightning, his red cape for power, and his winged helmet for tornados; and Benoit as a decayed tooth, with his body and arms as molar roots, a huge hollow head in an enamel crown eaten into by black, the cavity. Benoit complained of his pain, and people, laughing, gave him candy. Like all the youngsters, he carried around a moneybox to collect change for Unicef.

"I'm giving them one more chance," he said, "but if there are still famines next year, I'm going down to New York with a gun to make them get off their butts."

On my end, people wondered where I was coming from with my wool wraparound beard, my hair straightened with gel, my jacket and tie, a pen in my hand. I kept it all to myself until Monsieur Charbonneau's house, he was the French teacher, and there I handed him a card I'd rigged up at home. He read it and cried out:

"Solzhenitsyn!"

"Himself."

He was so beside himself that he called out to his wife at the top of his voice.

"Claudette! Bring me the camera! There's someone here dressed up as Solzhenitsyn!"

Monsieur Charbonneau was so impressed, and he so much wanted to please me that he went to find a book by Solzhenitsyn in his library.

"Here." He said, "a present."

The camera's flash blinded me just as I was reading the title: *One Day in the Life of Ivan Denisovich*.

That night, in my room, I devoured the book in a few hours, my first Solzhenitsyn, and even if I didn't understand everything, since it was a novel about a man who was older and more intelligent than me, and had been rewritten in a strange French by a translator in Paris, I still understood the tragic life of prisoner CH-854 in brigade 104, in a Russian work camp in the winter of 1952, and every page took me back to my friend Habéké, who I saw as a kind of African Ivan Denisovich, lost far off in a glacial world, behind rolls of barbed wire and watch towers, under the machine guns of brutal guards, in his reform school.

> *Since he'd had no bread at breakfast and what he'd eaten was cold, Shukhov felt really hungry today. And to keep his belly from whining and asking for food, he stopped thinking about the camp and thought instead about that letter he'd soon be sending home.*

That night, Halloween night, a first snow fell on our town like vinegar onto our wounds.

> *Dear Habéké,*
>   *I've just read a book by Solzhenitsyn and you were everywhere in those pages, in the wretchedness of Ivan Denisovich, and I'm afraid for you because it's written that there are those who have a healthy mouth and others that are rotted out, and that for a beaten dog it's enough to show him the whip, and that if you complain they break your back, that the moon is the wolf's sun, and...*

The pen fell from my fingers, and what I then saw in my sleep was me afloat on icy waters, on my bed, a ship with sheets as sails. The frigid wind was striking my face and tearing at my pyjamas, lifting me and sending me into the night through the open window. Off the world's seacoast waves battered me, and I flew over the dusty garden before veering toward the street in the haunted night, where small monsters left behind their trail's lace on a white sidewalk. It was like a snail ballet on sand, and I was sailing on a sky of snow, between streetlights, with beneath my bed thousands of shiny, tiny fish following me, downing cookie crumbs dropping from my blankets, and far off, over clear water, I knew my friends. I cried to them in the night, but those calls foundered in the ocean, yet I cried to them again, but the winds lost me in the infinite where my vessel burst apart and where I died, frozen hard over the white cadaver of my life's grandest dream.

*

IN NOVEMBER Odile turned sixteen, and she left school, which she had been attending only every other day. She didn't just leave school, but also her home and her former life, since she'd discovered something like love in the arms of a lout, a fair-haired Oaf with blue eyes. Odile took off without leaving an address, but I was able, one day, by leaning on Marie-France Bastien, to ferret out the locale of her newborn secrets. I went there on my bicycle one night, when it wasn't too cold and there wasn't too much snow on the streets, but it was quite far, out near the river. Odile lived there, on a dirt road that lost itself in a wind-battered field where large sickly elms went to die. She was living in an isolated mobile home, with her twenty-one-year-old Oaf who did nothing all day long.

I went there, but stayed out of sight, hidden by the dark.

"Send me her photo," Habéké wrote me one day. He was stark raving mad: he still loved Odile, blamed her for nothing because it was human weakness he said, and he had great respect for the weakness of men, even more for that of women. Far off in his reform school, Habéké still believed not only in love, but also in the miracles that would save Nathalie. He dreamed more than ever of our exile, he thought about it to the point of losing his mind, day and night, and he saw an enormous sun shining over the sea that was all that remained of Ityopia in his life. In his isle of madness there lived his sister, Zaoditou, his father and mother, his grandparents and his clan, all alive including Mekkonen, the restored dedjené, among the good spirits and the totems, and Habéké wrote me letters alive with fire that scorched my fingers and eyes, and I saw that no one could ever lock away Africas aflame.

You cannot lock away a sky: it's the sky that locks us away and puts us to death.

> *Dear Habéké,*
> *From the top of the big bridge, the one that crosses the river near where Odile lives, but really from the highest point of the bridge, in good weather, you can see on the horizon, in the middle of the river, a blue dot that seems to be a deserted island...*

Suddenly it was winter. A stunning flame lit up the skies, the comet Kohoutek, and Habéké wrote me that at night, huddled in his bed, he was petrified by this great shooting star that seemed to be inseminating the cosmos but was perhaps heralding catastrophes, the earth falling into the sun and the boiling of seas, famines, droughts, epidemics, or the vanishing of Africa into the abyss of Eritrea with its bubbling lava: or it was perhaps Mekkonen's soul going off to die among the distant stars. He scared me, Habéké, with his cataclysmic letters, and I destroyed them, all the ones where the evil comet is posing a threat to us—but not to the universe. I am weak, and I could never, with my naked hands, slow those blazing worlds that skim past us and rip away our souls.

> *Dear Habéké,*
> *I am the mortal comet that spears the heart and I am telling you that it is too late, that it's over, that we will never know Schla Maryam...*

Comets are dangerous talismans, closeted in dreams by the spirits of death; the harmattans of the sky bear away the souls of sick young girls into the eternal night. And in the wake of Nathalie, gone forever, another wind of affliction has swept over my life this winter, like something aching out of the depths of the universe, come to bury in my heart a shuddering of worlds.

> *Dear friends, Habéké and Hugues,*
>   *Our river will never reach the sea, nor any lake, nor any vast sheet of water. A river that ends in the sands! A river that empties out nowhere, that liberally bestows its purest waters, its utmost strength, just like that, along its path, and from time to time, directly to its friends. The very best thing we have ever known is a stretch of water where we were not desiccated, not yet, and where all that is left of us is the water we can hold in the palms of two hands, what we have offered of ourselves in an exchange with another, in an encounter, a conversation, an act of assistance.*
>
>   *Be well,*
>   *Alexander Solzhenitsyn*

Our letter had reached him through who knows what miracle, across seas and mountains, our spiritual father had answered us and I was overwhelmed. But it was too late, and I burned this letter.

> *Dear Habéké,*
>   *I am not certain, but if I understand well, I think we are dead.*

One night, the comet Kohoutek vanished from the skies, taking with it in its hair Nathalie's soul, but a bit of the comet's milk had flowed onto the earth to inseminate a young woman and leave in her womb a child imbued with the soul of scourges, a child of hypocrisy and the adult era, the child Odile carried, oh Odile my apocalypse, my Odile once so beautiful and pure, our Odile made pregnant by the Oaf.

Nineteen

WINTER HAD PASSED over the world, but its pain remained with me. Spring returned like an ever-deeper sadness, then summer burned my eyes. Céline and Claude didn't know what to do with me: I had no more friends and I lived shut up in my room, except at night when at times I rode my bike to Odile's, where she was awaiting her child, and to Nathalie's house, where I wept for her soul.

I never visited Habéké's parents. I blamed them too much for not having tried to plumb the depths of their adopted son, not having wanted to become Africans instead of turning Habéké into a Canadian, something that would have enabled them to better defend him against the Accident that wants only to grind up foreign souls; but in truth that's what they wanted, to grind him up, to scrub away all his black skin all the way to his blood and his bone, to uproot by force this supernatural universe that haunted him. But in ripping this evil out through his head, all the deep roots came with it, savaging Habéké to death.

Dear Habéké,

Summer is scorching the city and I am all alone. It's so hot that I'm spending my days in the basement where I can see that this can only go on and on. I no longer want to live in a world of madmen where everyone is afraid of everything, where no one believes in anything anymore, or loves life, and now the waters have burst, yes, Odile has brought forth the comet's child, but I still dream of exile, our beautiful exile at the sky's end and the seas that await us, but I will not leave without you, I'm waiting for you...

Habéké too had had enough of this savage world where everyone dreamed of killing him, of cutting off his black head and tearing out his heart to see if he pissed black blood, and I felt rising in him worlds filled with storms. His letters proliferated as his release from the reform school approached, they were shorter, sometimes just a few lines, but much more numerous, almost one a day, and when I scattered them over the carpet, I was impressed.

Dear Hugues,

That's it, I'm being let out tomorrow, September 1, just in time for school, and they've awarded me the gift of a month of my life, a truncated dozen. I think they believe I'll be going back to school, but I'm done with that and I'm coming, I'm on my way, prepare yourself because I'm ready and I'm not waiting one more day...

Twenty

To take one's leave rather than to die, because to leave is a bit like being born. Born by the skin of your teeth and your buttocks' skin like bastard children, or born into silk and jewels like princes: but prince or bastard, you have to be born if you want one day to die.

When Habéké resurfaced in the bright sunlight, all reformed and sanitized after his hard youth, I found that he'd grown and he found that I'd grown. I wondered what he saw in my eyes, but what I saw in his was the future. I remember that we went into the park near the arena and that he walked beside me like something strange dropped from the sky, as if I had thought him dead forever, dead physically, and he had suddenly surprised me by materializing in the light; and he seemed uneasy to be taking in so much light with his skin, he seemed anxious, on the alert, always tending to look back over his shoulder. We drank water from a fountain and sat on a bench, but we didn't have much to say to each other. He asked me the only important question.

"Are you ready?"

"I'm ready."

I'd thought of everything, and the plan was seared into my brain.

That night we made one last foray into the town where we had lived, and where we met. We hopped on our bicycles and rode to the school, gazing at it for a long time, then we left and turned onto rue Lanthier where Odile had lived. After that we rode along the railway all the way to the marshalling yards, but Habéké didn't have it in him to pass in front of our late friend's house, so we went back to the old garage at the back of my yard. We stayed there a long time, silent, sitting under a naked bulb, and by the time we separated, we knew it was going to be our last night in that world.

*

GOOD GOD, I was mad, yes, I would say I was mad all night long and even a bit longer. I felt the breath of life on my skin, this world I saw beyond the world was not what I had hoped for, yet still I had eyes to see, and I never stopped rooting through the nights whirling around me, seeing that they were there, those for whom I was alive were there in one of them and one day I would gain access to the good night I sought and I would live.

*

WE SPED AWAY in the chill morning, warmly dressed, on our bicycles. Before leaving I had taken one last glance into my semi-parents' bedroom to send them a final silent farewell, I slipped into Jasmine and Benjamin's to embrace them, then I petted Pipo and took off.

Habéké had pinned his farewell letter onto his pillow.

... one fine day the day will come when the authen-
tic unseen life will awaken and that day has come
for me and that's why this morning you will find my
bed empty...

My hands were white from gripping the handlebars so tightly, and I felt as if I were being swallowed up by time and space. When we came in view of Odile's, we stopped on a bridge along the dirt road. Seeing that we were alone, we thrust our bicycles into the stream and plunged into the bushes. Far off under a sickly elm, we spotted the Oaf and my blood went cold. Alone behind the house where laundry wafted on a line, his blonde head was buried inside the hood of his car and he was fiddling with its engine. I was holding on tightly to Habéké's baseball bat. When we felt ready, we came out of the bushes and approached the mobile home. Then we separated. As Habéké charged straight at the Oaf, cutting through the fields, I circled the house. When I emerged on the other side I saw him from the back, the Oaf, who had stood up to shout at Habéké. I took another few steps and found myself right behind him, and then, in one sweeping swing I hit him in the back of his head with the bat, and the Oaf crumpled. I didn't know whether I'd killed him, but he was bleeding and still, and the bat fell from my hands. I felt my legs go limp, my eyes fog up. I was someone's apocalypse, and sick to my stomach.

Then in a hazy dream I now see us, Habéké and me, bursting into the house where Odile was folding laundry in the bathroom, deafened by the washing machine. For a few seconds I thought she was someone I didn't know, another older woman, but then she moved and this movement of her arm overwhelmed me because it was her arm, and then I recognized her dark hair, the perfect profile of her face, her pale hands smoothing blouses. I don't know why, but for a moment

148

I felt as if I didn't exist, that I was not physically there, that I was an invisible spirit, that Odile would turn around without seeing me and I would remain there forever, admiring her. But out of the corner of her eye she saw shadows and she turned, her eyes wild, and as tears burned my throat I jumped on her with Habéké to gag her and tie up her legs and her fists. It pained me to see the hatred in her eyes.

"Don't be afraid," I said, "you're coming with us into exile."

Afterwards we went through the house, and found, in a basket at the back of a room, the comet's child. Very small and pale, he was brandishing a plastic rattle, and Habéké wrenched this dangerous talisman from his hands to shatter it on the ground. The child began to protest, but it was the soul of scourges that was showing itself. If he wanted to one day conquer the evil that dwelt within him, and to be reborn into the light, baptized with a new and powerful name, he had to shed all his body's tears, all his poisoned blood, and to suffer in solitude and despair for a long time. He would perhaps not survive this ordeal but it was his only chance to be transformed into a child of Good and of Justice, to perhaps one day save the world, but it would be this world we were leaving, not the world where we were going, given that this child belonged on this side of things, while we, Odile, Habéké, and I, were preparing to pass on to the other.

And so Habéké went to blindfold the mother by tying a towel over her eyes, poor Odile moaning and bucking like a fish upon the floor. Only then did I lift the child up to slide it into the wicker basket that was their container for dirty laundry, after which I ran to the end of a dock at the water's edge behind the house, where I set the basket afloat with the baby yowling inside it, and with my foot pushed it into the open water, into the current's eddy. Oh little baby, I thought, if it is your fate to survive you will survive, if it is to dazzle the world you will dazzle it. He perhaps had only one chance in a million to survive, but he would seize this opportunity if the good spirits and the good genies were with him. I thought that one day, perhaps, this miracle child with the comet's mane would save the world we were abandoning. It was not impossible, it was perhaps Him, but no one yet knew, seeing that a Christ must begin by dying if he wants to be reborn.

At which point I rejoined Habéké in front of the house where there was a wooden barrel I had spotted some time ago and which was part of our plan, a barrel painted all in white to make it pretty, wherein Odile had placed pots of flowers. We tossed the flowers into the ditch and rolled the barrel to the water's edge. Then we went back to get Odile and carried her in our arms, stepping over the Oaf, who was stirring a little in his blood. Once at the river's edge, we looked at each other, Habéké and I, then we set our eyes on the blue dot at the horizon, toward the island of exile where we would remake the world, where we would await all the spirits, our true families, the elder Mekkonen, the dedjené and the totems, the tatagu kononi, and the balanzas, and finally the living soul of Nathalie beneath the tree of life. We knew the hour of truth had come at last, that our dreamed-of world was atremble at the ends of our fingers.

But we still had to get there, to our fingers' ends, and we began by laying the barrel down to slide Odile into it feet first, then placing it upright, taking it to the water, and dragging it to the end of the dock, where Habéké in his turn got into it. The barrel was already half-way sunken, and I got in last, pushing off with my trailing leg, and that's how the barrel took to the water, floating erect like a buoy. Odile was stuffed in at the bottom, with Habéké and I over her on our knees. To have a little light, I'd placed the cover over our heads at an angle. Big as the barrel was, we were cramped and smothering, but this was just a difficult time to get through: we would soon land on our promised island, there, in exile, but then we saw water leaking in. First it was drop by drop, an oozing from between the planks, but then it began to trickle and stream, and Odile started to struggle and fight for air. We were sponging the barrel's bottom with our sweaters when we were hit by a powerful current that rolled us around. We turned about in the waves, volleys of cold water fell on our heads, and I began to long for us to land on one of our island's beaches. Suddenly we hit some rocks that thrust their spurs into the barrel like so many hatchet blows, and the river water spurted in through gashes in the sides. Then we crashed against another rock. Everything came apart from the force of that collision, and we were spat out into the current and I saw in a flash that all was lost.

Whirlpools gripped me and I could no longer see a thing, except a pale little sun, an end-of-life sun that shimmered in the froth. There were mysterious forces at work all around me, forces of death and forgetfulness, perhaps stemming from a time before birth, and that were wrenching us back toward that night of all beginnings.

A bridge support suddenly came into sight, and I grabbed onto it.

"Odile!... Habéké!..."

My friends didn't answer, and I kept on shouting for I don't know how long. After a while, I don't know when or why, I saw that I would henceforth be a man alone. My last hope was that Odile and Habéké would be washed up on our island of exile or on the shores of Africa, alive perhaps, perhaps in love one with the other.

I don't know what there is in love that has one wishing to know it, but I wanted it, yes, I wanted it for them, and today, somewhere, perhaps they have found it.

After the shipwreck I ought to have let myself founder in my turn, but I started to swim, not knowing why. Although I was weakened and found myself far from shore, I managed to reach a swamp where I dragged myself through the reeds. At the end of my strength and depleted by solitude, I started to shiver, curled into myself.

That is when a wailing reached my ears. I raised my head and went back into the water, wading toward the complaint on the opposite side of the swamp, where I parted the reeds. The comet's child was there. Its little fists trembled, and he was weeping in his basket of soiled clothes, adrift in the grasses.

I bent down, took him in my arms, and consoled him, whispering that he was an orphan and that he would have a long road ahead of him.

I watched him cry; inside his cheeks a lily of the valley was in flower.